MEET DAN

Dan Track grew up in a world where he had to fight in the streets for every inch of turf he wanted to call home. Fifteen years in the U.S. Army's Criminal Investigation Division battling gunrunners, terrorists, saboteurs and puppet dictators had taught him that the world didn't change—the stakes got higher, but the game remained the same.

In the Army, Track had seen postings in Germany, Japan, and in Saigon, where he'd found out just how dirty a dirty war could be. He became a master weapons specialist and a survival expert. He had no other choice.

At a well-muscled six feet with brown hair and steely gray-blue eyes, women find Track attractive, find his presence magnetic. But when he's not in the arms of a sexy arms smuggler named Desiree Goth, Track prefers the solitude of his place in New Mexico, where he can pull his thoughts together, test some guns and prepare himself for what always lies ahead.

Dan Track is a man dedicated to a single proposition: All men might be created equal, but one man *can* make a difference.

TRACK

The Ninety-Nine

JERRY AHERN

A GOLD EAGLE BOOK FROM

W⦿RLDWIDE

TORONTO · NEW YORK · LONDON · PARIS
AMSTERDAM · STOCKHOLM · HAMBURG
ATHENS · MILAN · TOKYO · SYDNEY

For Sharon, Jason and Samantha —
words never say enough. Love . . .

First edition June 1984

ISBN 0-373-62001-2

Printed in Canada

PROLOGUE

He had felt the gun under her pillow during the night when he had leaned her back, his fingers knotted in the blackness of her hair. But there had been other things, then, occupying his attention besides the gun—two thirty-eights rather than one. A .38 Special really had a .357-inch-diameter bore, closer to a .36.

He looked past the muzzle of the little stainless-steel Chiefs trained unwaveringly on him. The satin sheet only partially covered her, outlining her more. In the sunlight that streamed through the billowing sheers over the French doors leading from Desiree Goth's bedroom to her balcony, he reappraised the girl, as well as the gun. She, too, was closer to a thirty-six.

He smiled. "Breakfast in bed I can accept. Target practice in bed is a little kinky for me." His left hand was still under the sheet, and he reached out with it, grabbing at her. She screamed a little as he pinched her, his right hand snaking out to swat cross-body at the revolver. It wasn't cocked, anyway, and J-Frame Smiths usually have a hard trigger-pull. His right hand smothered the revolver; his little finger pinched between the hammer strut and the frame as the cylinder rolled against his palm. The girl double-actioned the revolver.

His left hand pushed up from under the sheet as he threw his body weight across her, his left hand clamping tightly over her mouth. "If you don't let go of that gun, I'll get a blood blister," he told her. "Now let go of the gun. Do it," he snapped, his finger really hurting him.

Her pansy-blue eyes were wide, startled, clear. "You're beautiful. Desiree—it means 'desired' in French, doesn't it?"

She let go of the gun. Track moved his right hand down and cross-body again, the gun still clinging to his little finger. It was going to form a blister. He edged the revolver against his right thigh, the hammer against his flesh. He dug the hammer spur in, moving the revolver. The hammer came to full stand with a click audible over the faint rustling of the sheers, the breathing of the woman.

He moved the gun away from his thigh, his finger still interposed between hammer and frame, the muzzle pointing toward the box spring beneath them both. The girl was moving under him now, anger replacing the startlement in her eyes as he glanced at her.

Track slipped his finger from between the hammer and frame, then rearranged his grip on the little revolver. His thumb was against the hammer spur now, his first finger edging against the grooves of the trigger. He tripped the trigger until the hammer started to move down, then eased the trigger forward so the rebounding firing pin wouldn't make it through the frame.

The hammer was down. "That feels better," he rasped. "My finger's gonna hurt."

She let out a muffled grunt.

"I'll take my hand off your mouth if you promise not to scream. I don't think it's part of a tough-guy image to punch a woman, but I'll do it, anyway."

She blinked, her lashes naturally dark and long like

the wings of some exotic butterfly, fluttering closed, then opening again. He felt her trying to nod her head under the pressure of his left hand.

"Remember, no screaming," he warned, and she nodded again. Track moved his hand slowly away from her mouth, resting it—gently, he hoped—around her long graceful throat.

She was breathing hard. "It's Major—Major Track," she panted, "isn't it?"

"Let me guess, my shoes were too shiny." He feigned a puzzled look. "Can't be the haircut. I leave it a little long just so I won't look military."

"CID. You're after me. What did you want me for last night?"

Her voice was a warm alto. He liked altos.

"I wanted to find out about the theft at the Wiesbaden arsenal, but it turned into something else. You're a beautiful woman, incredibly beautiful."

"Bullshit," she said, glaring at him.

"You are. Sounds stupid, but I just couldn't help myself. We were introduced. We had that drink. Then you danced with me. I haven't felt that way since I was thirteen."

"Thirteen?"

"I was precocious," he almost whispered.

"My men are outside. They've been there all night," she continued, breathing hard. "You'll never get out of here alive."

"You watch too many old movies, kid, but so do I. I have a gun at your head. They'll let me out."

"You wouldn't shoot me in the head."

"Don't count on it, sweetheart."

"I looked at you this morning when I woke up. I

started to bend over and kiss you. Then I remembered your face. All last night I thought I'd seen you before. It was last year, in Cortina.''

"Hjelstrom, the guy who was selling NATO explosives to the Red Brigades." Track smiled. "Yeah, I saw you, too, come to think of it. Small world, huh?''

"My man Zulu will kill you."

"You're scaring me."

"You came to arrest me, didn't you?"

"Not really, but I will now. There's a safe behind that picture over the bed," he told her. "Saw it before you killed the bedside lamp last night. Bet that's where you keep your records."

"You'll never know," she said, and smiled, her lips full, her mouth wide, a warmth to the smile that seemed out of place to him.

"Are they in there?" he asked. "Records that could put you away?''

She nodded. Track felt the movement of her throat as she swallowed. "But even if you beat me and get me to open the safe, you'll still never get out of here alive.''

"I don't know the kind of guys you hang around with, but where I come from you don't beat women. You only cold-cock 'em—you'll pardon the expression—and only if you have to. No, I'll get the authorities here, and they'll open your safe. Might be easier on the wallpaper if you give them the combination, though.''

"Bastard!" she snapped.

He shrugged. "We have to get out of bed now. I have to keep an eye on you while we dress. Sorry.''

She closed her eyes briefly, then opened them.

"No screaming?''

She shook her head. "I won't have to.''

"Right," he told her, easing his body weight from her, rolling back, the gun still in his right hand.

She stood up, swinging her long legs over the left side of the bed, then walked slowly toward the closet.

"Wait," he ordered, getting up, feeling oddly self-conscious and suddenly naked. He dressed hurriedly then stepped beside the closet, opening the door.

"I don't keep guns in the closet."

He gestured with the little stainless Chiefs.

She said nothing.

The closet stretched along an entire wall, some fifteen feet long, he judged. There were dresses, slacks, blouses, jackets—every color he'd ever seen and some he hadn't. "You want me to pick? Bet you look good in navy."

"That coat, the fox—" He reached across her with his left hand, keeping the right with the gun away from her as he did. He took down the coat and handed it to her, the fur soft against his fist. She shrugged into the coat, closing it around her, hugging herself in it. He knew from the weight there wasn't a gun in the pocket.

"I'm ready," she smiled, stepping into a pair of black high heels beside the closet door.

He felt slightly crawly not having taken a shower—and crawlier still when he'd tried the phone in Desiree's room beside the bed on the nightstand. The line had been dead.

Track started through the doorway into the hall, the girl's Chiefs Special the only weapon he had. There'd been no time to search the room for anything else, and dividing his attention between her and a search would have been inviting disaster.

Track's stomach rumbled. Desiree looked at him, raising her eyebrows.

"Sorry," he smiled as he glanced at the black-faced Rolex Sea Dweller on his left wrist. "Past breakfast time."

"An expensive watch for someone who's essentially a policeman. Do you take bribes?"

"Nope, but I'm running a special on sexual favors this week," he replied, grinning. She started to raise her right hand to slap him. He jabbed the muzzle of the Chiefs Special against her rib cage through the mid-calf-length fur coat.

They started down the hallway together. Track glanced at the expensive-looking, gold-leaf pattern on the walls. "You do all right for a gunrunner and smuggler," he told her.

"It's always chancy, working for yourself," she answered.

Something ran past his left foot. Track froze.

He looked down, shifting the revolver away from her for an instant.

It was a black cat. Desiree Goth wrapped the fur coat more closely around her as she stooped, stroking the animal as it arched its back and rubbed against her legs.

"You like cats?" Track asked her.

"This one," she said, smiling up at him. The color of her eyes seemed to match the cat's—the animal's were an unnatural blue. Their fur was nearly the same, he noted, also. Shining, healthy, black.

"I like cats, too. I'm leaving the military within the month to work privately as a weapons and tactics instructor. I've been doing it on my leave time for the past few years, teaching at one of the universities on weekends—police science. I've done some writing, as well. I'm going to give civilian life a try. Haven't for fourteen—no, fifteen—years. I'll get a cat. I like cats.''

"I like a man who likes cats," came the soft alto. Desiree Goth picked up the cat, stroking it. The animal purred, its tail moving slowly from side to side.

"I'd like to wait for you when you get out of prison, but we'd both be too old."

"You don't have to open my safe," she said, her voice low.

"You didn't have to rob the Wiesbaden arsenal."

"But the United States government has so many M-10s and LAW rockets," she began, the alto richer as she started to laugh. "Who's going to miss them?"

Track shrugged. "My colonel will. I'm supposed to get them back."

"You're certain?" she asked, still stroking the cat.

"I'm certain," he replied, nodding. "Sorry." And in that instant he felt he genuinely was.

Then she threw the cat in his face. The animal shrieked and spit, its claws gouging his face and neck. His left hand grabbed the cat by a handful of fur and flesh, ripping the animal away. Track winced as its claws came loose. He threw the cat down, then half stumbled over it as he chased the fleeing woman down the hallway. She turned the corner that led to the staircase down to the château's first floor. He skidded on his heels but quickly regained his balance.

Suddenly Track stopped.

A huge black man wearing a white T-shirt with a yellow smile face on the chest—it read Have a Nice Day—was swinging something that looked like a riot shotgun in his ham-sized fists. A blur came crashing down as

Track punched the little revolver forward. He felt a stab of pain, then felt nothing at all. . . .

TRACK OPENED HIS EYES, quickly closing them again against the sunlight streaming in through a round window. He was confused. He felt something touching his face, and he opened his eyes again. He moved his right hand quickly, grabbing a wrist—a small wrist. He focused. The wrist led to an arm that was part of Desiree Goth. The fur coat was gone, replaced by a khaki, short-sleeved bush jacket. Her eyes were smiling.

"Major Track—"

"Everybody calls me 'Dan,' " he told her.

"I remember. . . last night when we danced. . . you told me the same thing."

He nodded. He winced, his head aching.

"Nasty bump." He let go of her wrist and felt her hand prodding at the top of his head on the right near his hairline. Her hand stopped moving. "I like dark brown hair," she told him. "Most men take such terrible care of their hair."

He looked past her for the first time and saw the big black man with the ham-sized hands. Suddenly it came to him—the man who'd slugged him the night before was listed in Desiree Goth's CID file as her personal bodyguard. The only name in the file was Zulu. "Let me guess. He asked you for my scalp to hang on his spear."

Zulu's eyes didn't flicker. Desiree's did. "Zulu's an Oxford graduate," she explained. "He just happens to prefer guarding my body to teaching economics."

He winced when she touched his face. "Lie still," she said. "I'm fixing your face where Isabelle scratched you." As she dabbed at his face—whatever it was she was using stung briefly, then seemed to cool him—he listened. He heard a droning noise—aircraft noise, he guessed...a prop plane.

He turned his head slightly, looking past Zulu and seeing the forward section of a decent-sized private plane. The pilot was visible through an open curtain. He could see the glaring blue brightness through the windshield.

He looked past her hands, then back to her face.

"Beechcraft?"

She nodded, surprised. "How did you guess?"

"Read the buckle on the seat belt," he told her.

She laughed.

"Why do you care about my face? You're gonna kill me, right?"

"I'm very fond of you—for a reason I don't even understand myself," she told him. Her voice sounded somehow different to him—less well modulated, less rehearsed. "But business is business. There's no sense rushing it...your being in any pain before I have Zulu do it. And who knows? Maybe I can change your mind about opening my safe."

"The pilot—where's he taking us?"

"Captain Fulsom's flying us into the North African desert to keep a rendezvous with Ahmed Akbar and his men. I understand the Melek tribesmen are particularly interested in Ahmed Akbar not receiving his little shipment."

Track looked out the cabin window. He saw another aircraft. He leaned forward, seeing another and still another, all flying in formation.

"There are four cargo planes, plus our own aircraft,"

she explained, pulling him against the backrest. "Now lean back so I can finish your face."

"Ahmed Akbar's a terrorist."

"I know," she replied smugly.

"Why don't you turn these crates around, leave the weapons somewhere and I'll get you a deal—"

"You bargaining for your life?" she asked him, raising her eyebrows.

"You can't give this stuff to Ahmed Akbar. That's what I'm saying."

"I don't intend to 'give' this stuff to Ahmed Akbar, Dan. He's paying me for it."

Track shook his head. His head hurt. "Then sell it to somebody else. But not this son of a bitch. He's too bad, even for you, Desiree."

She leaned back, sighing. Track felt a change in the motion of the aircraft. He heard the hydraulics as the landing gear dropped, felt the slight shudder and heard the seat-belt sign ding on.

Track leaned forward and saw desert below them, coming up fast. Three gray black low tents—the center one substantially larger than the other two—loomed ahead and to starboard.

He looked at Desiree. "Zulu," she was saying, "keep an eye on Major Track. I don't want him dead yet." She stood up from the armrest where she'd perched, moving to the small table across the aisle and sitting down, crossing her jodhpur-clad legs. The nearly knee-high brown boots gleamed as they caught the sun. She reached under the seat as she swiveled it slightly. He heard a clicking sound—the seat locking—as he watched. She fastened her seat belt and turned away from him, staring out her window.

Track looked up at Zulu. The black man, changed from the smile *T*-shirt to no shirt at all and a pair of Levi's and sandals, was watching him. The man's body didn't move except for the easy rising and falling of his chest as he breathed; Track could see his muscles rippling.

"Aren't you going to fasten your seat belt?"

Zulu said nothing.

"Man, if this were a commercial airliner, you'd be in trouble now," Track commented, smiling.

Zulu did not smile.

TRACK STEPPED OUT onto the small foldout steps, following Desiree into the blistering heat. Dark clouds hung low on the far horizon near the foothills. He knew Zulu was immediately behind him; he could hear the steps creaking from the weight of the big man.

"I wouldn't advise, Dan," Desiree said, turning to Track, "that you let Ahmed Akbar know you're with the United States Army, much less CID. He might become upset and want to kill you himself. When the time comes—" she stopped at the base of the steps, looking up at him, her eyes bluer under the brim of the theatrical-looking pith helmet "—I'll just have Zulu shoot you fatally. It'll be over quickly. With Ahmed Akbar it wouldn't."

"Thanks for the tip," he said, stepping down into the hard-packed sand of the dry lake bed beside her. He looked back, watching Zulu. The big black was clutching a shotgun—a Remington 870 with a twenty-inch slug barrel and rifled sights, sling swivels and a Safariland Velcro sling and add-ons such as the extension magazine slightly ahead of the barrel and a salmon-colored elastic

Perry ammo sling bandaged onto the recoil-pad stock. Zulu also carried a pistol, in cross-draw fashion, midway between his left hipbone and his navel. The button of the navel was enormous. Track guessed the man had been born somewhere far from a hospital. The handgun was a Browning Hi-Power—indistinguishable from any other Hi-Power.

Track looked toward the murmuring noises he heard. He saw two dozen men dressed as Bedouins, their dark rough-cloth djellabas thrown on over embroidered *brussa* shirts. The men nearest to the front of the throng wore more ornately embroidered *brussas*, more intricately plaited *akal* headbands over the flowing *keffiyehs*. Those in the middle had on darker rougher cloth, and those to the rear carried assault rifles slung over shoulders or held sloppily at port arms.

A sudden wind sprang up. The sand stung Track's cheeks, reminding him of the scratches from the cat. As the Bedouins stopped less than five feet from him, Desiree Goth and Zulu, he decided that if he did survive, maybe he wouldn't get a cat.

"Mademoiselle Goth," a squat goateed man at the exact center of the Bedouins began, salaaming to her.

"The great Ahmed Akbar," Desiree Goth answered, nodding her head. Track watched her smile, feeling himself smile more broadly. The Bedouin who spoke was not Ahmed Akbar.

"I have brought this first shipment of weapons to you personally, Ahmed Akbar, but you should know this is far from my usual practice. In future dealings, my trusted associate—" she gestured limp-wristedly with her right hand to Zulu "—will represent my interests with you. But the honor of meeting the great Ahmed Akbar—"

she smiled again ""—far outweighs any inconvenience.""

The Arab bowed before her, then spoke once more. "I am a great student of religions. Yours has angels, and you speak with the tongue of one of those, Mademoiselle Goth."

She was acting. Track watched her at it—the downcast eyes, the demure smiles, the slightly pursed lips, then the eyes opening, as somehow, despite being three inches taller than the Bedouin in the high-heeled boots she wore, she seemed to be looking up at him. "Ahmed Akbar flatters me greatly."

Track muttered, "Crap."

"My cargo is about to become your cargo," she began again, looking at the man who called himself Ahmed Akbar.

"And my gold is about to become your gold." The Arab laughed broadly. "We shall adjourn to the center tent. We shall take tea, and there are dates. A pleasant respite from a wearisome journey while the weapons are unloaded and the gold brought forth." Then "Ahmed Akbar" bowed, his hand sweeping a path toward the central tent as the group of Bedouins—Track counted twenty-three—parted their wedge to make a gap. Desiree started forward, and Track felt Zulu prod him slightly with the riot shotgun.

Track whirled, then quailed at the sight of the gun in the huge black man's hands. He turned and continued walking. He reached abreast of Desiree Goth, trying to fall into stride with her, finding it impossible, then just walking more slowly to avoid getting ahead of her.

The Bedouins closed in behind him—he could feel them, see them from the corners of his eyes. The time on the Rolex read late afternoon—he had not yet eaten and thought the dates and tea didn't really sound that bad.

"Do you come here often?" Track asked, looking at a leathery-faced Bedouin near his right elbow. The man looked back at him, puzzled, not smiling. Track noticed the gun in the man's sash—a .45 automatic, probably stolen from U.S. inventory.

Track liked .45s.

"Your mother," he told the Bedouin, "had the hots for camels."

Still the Bedouin's expression didn't change. Track felt confident the man didn't speak English.

Track bent slightly toward Desiree's right side, his rasping whisper audible only to her, he hoped, and the Bedouin who spoke no English. "This guy isn't Ahmed Akbar. This is a setup," he singsonged to her.

She glanced at him, the sockets of her eyes widening to where they looked as if they would rip with the tension, rimming the blueness with white. "What?"

"I don't know who he is, but he isn't Ahmed Akbar."

"Liar," she snapped.

He pretended to trip slightly so he could kick her right shin with his left foot.

She winced, glaring at him then as they walked on across the dry lake bed toward the center tent, its flap open, the tent less than fifty yards from them now.

"You can hit me on the head, throw your damn cat in my face, have Zulu kill me, but don't call me a liar, or I'll wring your pretty neck," Track threatened.

Her eyes narrowed, then widened again. "What— what do—"

"What do we do?" He smiled, moving closer to her. The open tent flap, yawning dark at them, was less than a dozen yards away. "Tell Zulu not to kill me when I go for this guy's gun. Tell him to back my play. And you run like hell."

She nodded, turning away from him.

Above the low keen of the wind, the rustling sounds of the djellabas catching the rush of air, he heard a new sound. He had been in the country once as a boy, seen them as they crossed through the air in a black living cloud. Locusts. But there were no locusts, just the sound of locusts. Perhaps a buzzing of the lips made it, or a wailing from the throat. Like Indian war whoops, but somehow colder to hear, more chilling.

Track looked toward the foothills.

Horsemen, seeming ten feet tall as heat shimmered off their dark clothes and their dark, almost floating mounts. Rifles were raised high in the air above their heads.

He heard the murmuring behind him—a shout from the Bedouins surrounding them.

"Now that's Ahmed Akbar," Track shouted to Desiree. "Run for it!" He wheeled half right, his right elbow whipping up, hammering back and out. He heard the snap of bone. His left hand snaked toward the sash as the Bedouin beside him started to fall back. Track's left hand closed on the .45. The hammer was down.

He jerked the gun free of the sash, silently praying the chamber was loaded as he rammed the pistol out, thumbing back the hammer, pulling the trigger as one of the guards carrying an M-16 stepped through the wedge toward him, the assault rifle up.

The pistol bucked in his left fist. The Bedouin's face seemed to pucker inward, then explode, blood spraying in a cloud as Track stepped back two paces, switching the pistol to his right hand.

There was a loud boom, then another and another. Track looked up to see Desiree running; Zulu firing the riot shotgun from his hip, the muzzle rock steady and unmoving; six of the Bedouins down; another tumbling. Track pumped the trigger of the .45—another head shot. But he'd been aiming for the chest.

He started to run, hearing the Arab horsemen behind him now. He jammed the .45 into his waistband, then snatched up an M-16 from one of the dead Bedouins. They were Melek tribesmen, and this bogus Ahmed Akbar was one of them.

Track saw "Ahmed Akbar" running for the center tent as the walls of all three tents were ripped away from inside, armed men spilling from them.

"Hell," Track rasped, firing a burst from the M-16. Then he turned and ran.

He was in the middle of a war, he realized. The spoils of the battle were the shipment of arms aboard the planes.

He kept running, jumping the body of a dead Bedouin, pumping the M-16's trigger at the last of the group, who'd walked out to the Beechcraft alone. But heavy gunfire poured from the tents and from the horsemen of the real Ahmed Akbar.

Track wheeled, emptying the M-16 at the tents. The Melek tribesmen were closer, their gunfire more potentially deadly.

He saw Zulu running, and Track turned and ran after him, still gripping the empty M-16. Desiree was streaking across the dry lake bed toward the Beechcraft. The plane had started to taxi. And beyond the rim of the lake bed he could see more horsemen.

"Jeez," he shouted, throwing his arms out from his

sides as he clenched the M-16 in his right hand. He put his body into the run, sucking air hard. Zulu, ahead of him, ran effortlessly for such a big man.

Suddenly Zulu went down. Desiree looked back simultaneously.

It shocked Track—he hadn't expected it of her—but the woman turned, stumbled, then started heading for Zulu.

Track stole a glance behind him. The Bedouin horsemen of Ahmed Akbar were racing past the gray black tents now. The men were hunched low in their saddles, half obscured by the necks and flowing manes of the sweat-streaked animals as they bore down on him.

Track, like Desiree, kept running toward Zulu.

Then Track heard it—the sound of hooves close behind him. Wheeling, he saw the horseman pounding toward him. Track flipped the M-16, grabbing the barrel in midair and in the same motion swinging it hard. The buttstock of the rifle thudded dully against the rider, hurling the man from the saddle. Track reached for the riderless animal, but it reared, then bolted away.

Track wheeled again, his rifle lost in the swing. The Bedouin was scrambling to his feet. A long-bladed scimitar flashed under the rays of the desert sun, and the saber whistled toward Track. Track jumped back, whipping the .45 from his trouser belt. He dropped the thumb safety and jerked the trigger, keeping the muzzle low, since the gun shot so high.

But the gun didn't fire. Track dodged the slashing blade. The Bedouin seemed to jump skyward, landing like a cat. The sword arced again. Track jerked back the slide on the .45, snatching the chambered round in midair with his left hand. Sidestepping the Bedouin's blade, he glanced down at the cartridge—it was green with corrosion. "Hell," Track rasped, pumping the trigger of the .45. Nothing happened—again.

"Damn," he snarled. The flashing steel arced toward him yet again. He used the .45 now to block the sword. The blade skittered along the length of the slide toward his right fist, knocking the .45 loose. Track spun, snapping his left foot up and out—a double Tae Kwon-Doe kick to the Bedouin's left hip. The man stumbled back from the impact.

Track continued to circle another 180 degrees right; his right leg snapped up and out, sweeping toward the Bedouin's head. He missed, then wheeled again, back-kicking with his left toward the Arab's face. The Bedouin was falling, and the scimitar was spinning out of his hand. Recovering quickly, he snatched at Track's ankle with his left hand. Track dropped to the right; using his outstretched left leg to hook against the Bedouin's neck, pulling him down. Track executed a 360-degree roll on the dry lake bed, stomping his right foot out into the man's face, once, then once again. The Arab lay still.

Another Bedouin streaked across the sand toward Track, his sword held high. The sun, a bloody orb, was dropping now behind Track, its orange red light glinting on the steel that weaved toward him.

Track pushed himself up to his hands and knees, snapping both legs out, throwing himself against the horse's knees. The animal's hooves brushed against Track's shoulders and back, whistling past his head. The horse whinnied as it tumbled forward. Track moved to the left, his face sprayed with sand, his lungs choking on dust as the animal went down.

The Bedouin slipped from the saddle. The horse

rolled over on its back, wildly pawing the air as its rider jumped clear. Track was up, wiping dust from his mouth and face with the back of his right hand, stepping into the Bedouin as he rose. Track wheeled half right, his left foot snapping out with a single kick to the abdomen or groin. He wasn't sure what he hit, just of the impact. He wheeled 180 degrees right, and his right foot snapped out into the Bedouin's face. The Arab doubled forward.

Track finished the arc with his right leg, then regained his balance, half throwing himself forward across the Bedouin's body. Track's left hand snatched at the reins as the horse—a magnificent black Arabian, sweat glistening in the dying sun—stumbled to its feet.

Track had the reins. He pushed himself up and tugged the animal close to him before it could rear. Both hands reached out to the low-curving pommel of the cloth-covered saddle; Track's forearm muscles screamed as he hauled himself up into the saddle. The animal reared under Track as his feet found the stirrups. He jabbed his heels into its sides. The horse, its nostrils flaring, sprang forward.

Flecks of sweat and froth sprayed him as he bent low over the Arabian's neck. The flowing blackness of the mane—like Desiree's hair, but darker—swatted at him, slapping against his face.

Desiree—he could see her beside Zulu now—was trying to help the big man to stand.

"Hang on," he screamed, spurring the horse again with his heels. Track glanced behind him and saw more of the Bedouin horsemen of Ahmed Akbar. There was gunfire everywhere. He heard the whoosh of a LAW rocket to his left. Looking up, he saw one of the planes burst into flames as an orange-and-black fireball erupted skyward.

He started tugging back at the reins. The animal skidded under him. Track pitched forward in the saddle, straightening his legs as he threw his weight back. The Arabian slowed, stopped.

Track looked at Zulu—the man was enormous...perhaps two hundred fifty pounds. The animal wouldn't take the double weight.

Track jumped from the saddle, wrestling the animal forward by its reins, reaching for Zulu. "Get up here, you son of a bitch!"

The black man, his naked upper body glistening, red stained over his left shoulder with sand-clotted blood, glowered at him.

"Zulu, mount the animal," Desiree pleaded. "Track will look after me—hurry!"

The black man nodded soberly, then handed Track his gun. Track took it, still holding the prancing Arabian as Zulu, with Desiree pushing him, climbed into the saddle.

"I will stop Fulsom and the Beechcraft. We will wait for you," Zulu said emotionlessly, then held the reins as if he'd been born in the saddle. He drew back, and the horse reared.

Desiree hugged close to Track. The black Arabian with the black rider sprang ahead.

"Start running," said Track, turning to Desiree. He found the 870's slide release and worked the pump back a half inch or so to check for a chambered round, then moved it forward.

The Bedouin horsemen, now less than twenty yards away, were riding down on them. "Run," Track shouted after her, turning, shouldering the riot shotgun.

He fired once. The lead horseman went down. His animal seemed to scream as it skidded across the sand on its left flank.

Track dropped the shotgun to hip level and rammed the five rounds from the Perry sling, one at a time, into the magazine tube. He guessed blindly that the tube had six rounds left. He tromboned the pump, shouldered it again and sighted over the front blade. He fired, tromboned; fired, tromboned; fired, tromboned; fired.

He wheeled half left. Two of the nearest Bedouin horsemen broke off to outflank him. Their assault rifles spit orange tongues of flame, and the slugs kicked up sand at his feet. He tromboned the pump, fired—one horseman down; then tromboned the action again, firing—the second rider down. Track pumped the action, and the red high-brass shell sailed out of the ejection port. Nothing in the chamber.

A Bedouin rode down fast upon him. Track had no time to use the shotgun as a club. He flung it aside, at once hurling his body weight against the horse's neck. The horse stumbled, reared. Track fell back. The Bedouin rider spilled to the sand.

Track ran for the horse, grabbing at the reins. The animal reared again. Track found the mane and snatched handfuls of it. Settling the gray Arabian, he vaulted into the saddle.

The Bedouin rider was standing, bewildered. Track jerked the reins, making the animal rear under him. Wild-eyed, the Bedouin tried in vain to dodge the flying hooves of the pawing stallion in the loose sand. Track heard a crunch as the horse came down on the Arab, the top of his once white *keffiyeh* now splotched red with blood.

"Gyaagh!" Track screamed, and the animal bounded ahead of him.

He could see Desiree two hundred yards from the aircraft, which was now stopped. The black Arabian that Zulu had been riding was riderless. Track prayed Zulu had got aboard.

Crouching low over the horse's neck, Track rode, his heels flailing at the animal. Sweat and froth again bathed his face. Weaponless now, he looked over the saddle. A sword hilt protruded on the lower right behind the cantle.

Track reached for it, drawing the saber out of the sheath, using the blade flat against the Arabian's withers. The animal seemed to race still faster over the gray-and-tan streaked sand of the dry lake bed.

Two more horsemen were bearing down on Desiree; one reached out with a scimitar.

"Gyaagh!" Track dug in his heels, slapping the sword flat against the animal. Their shadow seemed to fly across the desert sand—they were as one.

The nearer of the two Bedouins—the one with the sword—was closing in on Desiree. Her little Chiefs glinted at the end of her rigidly extended arms. The gun belched a tongue of flame, and the Bedouin's horse swerved left. The Bedouin urged the animal ahead, his sword held back and high, ready to chop.

"Get outta my way!" Track shouted, interposing his mount between Desiree and the sword-wielding Bedouin. Track's mount reared, wheeled, reared again, as Track hacked out with the sword, locking it against the blade of the Bedouin's saber. The enemy's horse backed skillfully. The Arab was experienced at sword fighting from horseback, Track realized, a cold sick feeling in his stomach. As his horse wheeled under him, Track could see Desiree's little revolver bucking in her hands as the second Bedouin dropped from the saddle.

Track raised his blade, blocking a thrust from the first Bedouin, who came charging and screaming at him.

The Arab's mount suddenly stumbled as Track's blade hacked out in a wide arc. He felt the impact of steel slicing through flesh and gristle as the blow severed the Bedouin's head.

Track wheeled his horse, searching for Desiree. She watched him giving his mount its head. The Arabian was bearing down on her. She fell into a half crouch, her arms upraised, waiting.

Track rode toward her, flinging the sword away. He leaned low across the animal's neck, hooking out his right arm. The horse slowed momentarily on impact as Track swooped up the woman. Her hands locked around him as she swung astride.

He kept riding toward the aircraft.

Suddenly he heard thunder behind him.

"Riders, Dan, about two dozen of them!"

He looked back but watched the open doorway of the plane. He wondered what Zulu would do. He would do something; that was certain.

Then Track jerked the reins of his mount hard right. The horse's head craned against the pull, the muscles in its gray, froth-flecked neck rippling. The animal seemed to skid. Then it deflected right.

Zulu, his massive arms supporting an M-60 machine gun, was in the open doorway, firing.

Track's animal reared. Desiree's arms locked around Track tighter. He glanced hard right—the Bedouin cavalry was going down, wave after wave; assault rifles blazed skyward or emptied harmlessly into the sand. Horses were rearing, falling.

Track crouched low over his animal's neck, coaxing a final burst of speed from the laboring beast.

The animal's mane slapped him. Desiree held him tightly. Wind lashed his face.

"Gyaagh!" Fifty yards.

Twenty-five.

The plane had started to move slowly. Track reined in his mount as Desiree slid to the ground. He swung down and swatted the horse's rump with his right hand as he wheeled, grabbing Desiree's right hand in his left. Running toward the plane, they could see Zulu still firing the M-60 from the open doorway.

The backwash from the plane's props was spraying a fine sand into their faces. Desiree coughed and stumbled. Track caught her, and the girl was up and running beside him.

"Zulu, grab her!"

The black man let go of the gun, then dropped to his knees, reaching out for his charge as Track pushed Desiree ahead of him.

The corded muscles in Zulu's shoulders rippled as he grabbed her up like a rag doll. She was cradled in her bodyguard's arms for an instant, then thrust out of sight into the aircraft.

The plane's speed picked up.

"Shit!" Track snarled, running.

But Zulu was back in the doorway, reaching out again. Track was lifting his arms when a knife flashed into Zulu's hands, its steel catching the sunlight. The black's right arm snapped back for a throw.

"No, damn you!" Track screamed the words, his throat raw.

The blade left Zulu's right hand, and his arm snapped forward like a striking cobra. The knife whistled past Track and the steel came to rest in the chest of a Bedouin horseman.

Track half stumbled again, his lungs screaming for oxygen as he felt Zulu's fingers locking over his wrists.

His arms seemed to rip from their sockets as he was dragged up the steps into the plane.

He heard Zulu grunt. Then the massive black man stumbled back, blood spurting from a chest wound.

Track stumbled against the bulkhead, shouting to the pilot, "Fulsom, get this damned thing airborne, and quick!"

He looked behind him. Desiree was reaching into a closet in the forward bulkhead. The plane lurched as Track tried to keep his footing. Desiree was clutching an M-16.

"Dan, catch," she shouted as she tossed the gun to Track. He caught it deftly, his shoulders and back aching as his fist closed on it.

He eased back the bolt, swinging the muzzle outward through the open door. He braced his body against the frame, firing at the pursuing Bedouin horsemen. In the distance, on the far side of the lake bed, he could see all four cargo planes burning, flames licking skyward as LAW rockets and ammunition exploded.

"Track, the steps—" Fulsom shouted. "We can't take off!"

"Damn," Track snarled, looking down. The passenger steps for the door still hung open, plowing the sand.

Track threw the assault rifle onto a seat beside him. He found a seat belt and balled it around his fist. Then he swung himself down, reaching for the handle as the sand from the prop draft lacerated his flesh. Bedouin bullets ricocheted off the fuselage as he strained to retrieve the steps.

He had the handle, but the steps were stuck. He could feel his hand slipping from the seat belt.

Suddenly viselike grips locked on his right wrist and he felt his body being torn in two. Then the steps were free. They closed shut as he fell back into the aircraft.

He looked up to see Desiree at the door, working the lock. The rush of air was suddenly gone.

His right wrist felt as if it were broken. He realized the hands that had locked on his right wrist were Zulu's.

The man laughed loudly, sweat streaming down his face. Sweat, blood and sand dripped from his body.

"Miss Desiree—shall we kill him now?"

Incredulous, Track looked at the man, then at Desiree Goth.

She dropped to her knees, her arms going around Track's neck. She released him, then hugged Zulu. She broke away. The blood from his body smeared the front of her bush jacket.

Then she laughed, a real laugh—something Track had never seen her do.

"No evidence. It all blew up out there," Track rasped, still breathless.

"My safe?"

"What safe?" Track smiled.

"I love you—but if you bother me again, I'll kill

you.'' She threw her arms around him once more, her lips, warm and moist, crushing his.

His stomach lurched once, and Zulu laughed again. They were airborne.

Track kept kissing Desiree.

1

Klaus Gurnheim had always liked tinkering—especially with clocks. That had first led him, he reflected now as he hid, to bombs.

He heard footsteps crunching on the roof, slipping, then crunching closer. He drew the lockblade folding knife from the right hip pocket of his Levi's and waited.

He recognized the sound of metal scraping leather—the antiterrorist policeman had drawn his gun.

Gurnheim pressed himself flatter against the red brick of the chimney.

These men carried the H&K P-7, the squeeze-cocking 9mm. He heard a tiny mechanical click; the footsteps were getting closer now.

A voice, very near but below the roofline, asked, *"Was ist los?"* Then the same voice queried again, *"Was ist passiert?"*

From beside the chimney, inches from Gurnheim, came a reply, *"Es macht nichts, Fritz!"*

"Widerholen Sie!"

"Niemand, Fritz!" The near voice again.

Gurnheim held his breath, his knife not yet open.

The crunching started again. Suddenly the plain-clothes policeman came around the chimney, a startled look in his green eyes as he spotted Gurnheim.

One-handed, Gurnheim flicked open the lockblade,

ramming it forward into the red-haired policeman. The pistol discharged, but Gurnheim felt no pain. Gurnheim again rammed the knife into the officer's chest. The young man screamed, *"Meiner Brust! Fritz!"*

The pistol discharged once more. Gurnheim slipped, skidding on the peaked roof as he tried to reach for the gun. It clattered down the roof shingles, following the young officer as he rolled off the roof.

Gurnheim lost his balance. He slipped and tumbled forward.

He saw a rain gutter and frantically grabbed for its edge to stop his downward plunge. His fingers hurt as he held it. Then the gutter tore away, swinging out from the roofline. A gunshot. Another shot. His ears rang as one of the bullets punched into the rain gutter.

"Polizei!" shouted a voice from the ground.

Gurnheim hung from the gutter as it started to sink under his weight.

"Hilfe!" he shouted. *"Hilfe!"* He looked below him, dizzy. *"Schnell!"*

The policeman on the ground knelt beside his young red-haired colleague. The man was obviously dead.

Gurnheim heard a voice from the ground. The one who was apparently Fritz looked up, his pistol clenched in both fists. Gurnheim's eyes were riveted to the muzzle. But the words weren't for him. He looked farther along the street below. Uniformed police were running and shouting. *"Rufen Sie einen Krankenwagen. . . einen Krankenwagen!"*

Counterterrorists had discovered bombs and explosives in Gurnheim's apartment; he was wanted by the authorities in four European countries; he had just led the police in a six-block foot chase through the streets of

Hamburg. Now, as he hung by his hands from a collapsing rain gutter, he laughed.

But he stopped laughing. There was hate in the eyes of the young policeman, the one named Fritz, who held the gun pointed at him.

He had hung there for five minutes, he guessed. A fire ladder was raised beside him now as policemen cordoned off the area below him. Firemen were ready with a net. A lean-faced man with tousled brown hair, wearing an open khaki trench coat with a woolen muffler around his neck, ascended the ladder.

Gurnheim knew the face. It belonged to the Englishman assigned to work with the West German counter-terrorist units. His name was Durkey.

"You speak English, don't you?" the man said. Without waiting for an answer he said, "Of course you do, Gurnheim—terrorists are usually polyglots."

"Get me down, Durkey," Gurnheim snarled.

"Yes, I must get you down. Sad. I'd rather let you just hang until you drop. Then you could die, like that young policeman."

"Go to hell, Durkey!"

"You know us, don't you," the Englishman said, his voice low. "We won't let you just flop down there and die."

"It is your weakness," Gurnheim gasped, his back aching, his fingers numb. He doubted he could hold on any longer.

"Here, let me help," Durkey said. He reached out and grabbed Gurnheim's right ankle, placing his foot on a rung. Gurnheim released his hold on the gutter. Durkey grasped at his free right hand. Gurnheim was losing his grip with his left hand, falling, but something was holding him.

It was Durkey. The Englishman's left arm was threaded through the ladder rungs; both hands were clamped tight on Gurnheim's right wrist. Gurnheim swung there a moment. "Why—why don't you let me fall, kill me?" Gurnheim swung, watching the strain in the hard cheeks of the Englishman.

"You said it, Gurnheim—it is our weakness, isn't it?" and Gurnheim swung his left arm around to grasp at the ladder, Durkey never letting go.

GURNHEIM STOOD IN THE WITNESS DOCK, not having bothered with a lawyer. He knew what the verdict would be even as the judge droned on. For the bombing of the synagogue in Cologne that killed eighteen people; for the derailment by incendiary device of the train near Stuttgart when forty-seven died; for the airplane bombing out of Berlin that sent 280 to their deaths; for the dissemination of destructive devices to known terrorists; for the murder of the policeman—Gurnheim hadn't wasted his time to bother remembering the man's name—and for a long list Gurnheim had stopped listening to midway.

He heard the verdict.

He smiled. It could have been nothing else.

He watched Durkey's face. Someday, when he escaped, he would leave Durkey a nice "present" on the engine block of his car. Then the true escape would come.

Guilty, indeed.

DURKEY SEEMED TO WHISPER; Gurnheim only half listened to him. "It's an honor to be allowed to accompany you to prison, Gurnheim. To see you shut away."

Gurnheim said nothing.

"You might be able to have your sentence adjusted. Perhaps a more posh prison rather than the hole we're putting you in. Just tell us about Johannes Krieger."

Still Gurnheim said nothing.

"I know you probably don't know his face. No one does, we understand. He fancies himself a master of disguise, he does. But tell us what you know. If you do, we'll turn this car around and find you a better prison, give you a new identity. Plastic surgery, perhaps, so Krieger will never be able to find you."

Gurnheim remained silent, staring down at his manacled hands. The belly chain around his waist irritated him over the blue prison shirt he wore. His ankles were manacled, too. He sat on Durkey's right in the back seat. He stared at the back of the driver, then at the guard beside the driver in the front seat. Gurnheim's gaze traveled slowly sideways toward Durkey, who continued to speak.

"Why don't you consider it, Gurnheim? Because if you think Krieger can help you, you're insane. He cannot. A decoy car was sent out with a man dressed and built exactly like you. If Krieger puts together some sort of terrorist task force, he'll attack the wrong car. You'll still go to prison."

Again Gurnheim did not reply. He was waiting.

"Krieger is a butcher. What if we put it out on the street that you told us everything you knew, put you under maximum security but under your own name. It would be only a matter of time before he got you.

Krieger is very good. I'm offering you a choice—a false name in a better prison, or I can make you a sitting duck, as the Americans say. Would you like that?''

Gurnheim merely watched the scenery along the country road, slightly distorted through the bullet-resistant glass of the police car.

"What do you hope to achieve by silence? Is it loyalty to that bloody butcher?''

Gurnheim looked at Durkey, finally saying something. "Your conversation, Herr Durkey—it grows tiresome.''

Durkey's eyes hardened. "Look, you bastard, it can grow a good deal more tiresome for you in that prison. We'll be there in less than an hour. Think about that. And think about our letting it out that you spilled your guts, Gurnheim! Think about how tiresome that could get!''

Gurnheim said nothing more, shrugging his shoulders and returning his gaze to the distorted scenery.

Durkey spoke again. "Krieger is slime, Gurnheim, slime. A murderer of women and children. Hiding behind disguises, he's too afraid to show himself.''

"Herr Durkey, you are very tedious, indeed.'' Gurnheim sighed.

"Tedious? You fucking bloody bastard, I'll show you tedious.'' Durkey, his face livid, turned forward and reached across the front seat to the driver, tapping him on the shoulder. "Stop the car. Stop the bloody car!''

"But, Herr Inspector,'' the driver pleaded, half turning over his shoulder.

"Stop the bloody car, man!''

"But, Herr Inspector!''

"Take this bastard to his damned prison and pick me

up on the way back. I can't stand the smell! Stop, I tell you!''

"*Ja*, Herr Inspector." The driver nodded, pulling off to the side of the two-lane highway. Gurnheim was watching, interested.

"And you," Durkey shrieked. "You—you filth." He slapped Gurnheim. Gurnheim's head snapped back, and a thin trickle of blood started as his lip impacted against his teeth.

Both the driver and the guard beside him turned around at the sound of the slap. Durkey's wrists jabbed forward. His hands were cocked back at bizarre angles, and a clear liquid squirted out from beneath each wrist into the faces of the driver and the guard. Durkey—his voice somehow different—rasped, "Cyanide, Gurnheim!"

Gurnheim bent his head forward between his knees, covering his face with his manacled hands. In a blur of motion he saw Durkey's raincoated right arm reach past his face.

Gurnheim heard the click of the door lock beside him. He felt himself being shoved out onto the road. Then he landed on his right shoulder and hip.

He pushed himself up to his knees. Hearing a car door slam, he glanced up.

Still on his knees, he stared ahead at the raincoat of Inspector Durkey.

Gurnheim looked up as Durkey started to speak, but the inspector's voice was different somehow. "Really, Klaus, you are so loyal to me." Then the British accent again. "That Krieger, the slime, the butcher," and then the slight German inflection. A voice he knew—Krieger's. The man in the raincoat laughed. "That butcher has struck again, hasn't he, hmm? Cyanide gas and two dead pigs, *ja*?"

The laugh—Gurnheim had heard it before, though he'd never seen the face. Feeling confused, stupid, still on his knees, he stammered, "But, Johannes...Durkey, the *Engländer*...the counterterrorists—How—?"

"Durkey never quite completed the trip from London to Stuttgart. There was a tragic accident at Heathrow airport; the body was hidden. An easy matter to match the passport photo of a man no one in West Germany had ever seen."

"You—you on the ladder before the trial?"

"Why do you think I saved your bloody life, Klaus? For Durkey to do it he would have had to have been a bigger bloody ass than the police usually are. Been rather nice, actually, living as Durkey for the past nine weeks, reviewing all the counterterrorist files, mislaying a few interesting sets of fingerprints—such as my own. Which the ignorant swines never even knew they had in their possession! Ha." He laughed again, then fell silent.

Gurnheim, still kneeling, looked up as Krieger's hands reached out to his shoulders.

"You are loyal, Klaus Herman Gurnheim. This is something money cannot buy."

Gurnheim, feeling stupid for thinking it, felt somehow he was being knighted by Krieger.

"Get up, my friend—I shall help you." Krieger—his hands somehow irresistibly powerful—drew Gurnheim up until he was standing.

Gurnheim looked at his manacled hands.

"But Johannes—"

"These shackles—we will dispose of them soon.

There is a job... the rarest and best opportunity. And I need your expertise with the use of bombs, with timing devices. I need you. You will help?

"I will bring the United States, all the Western democracies and the Communist bastards, all of them, crawling on their knees. But no hands will reach out to uplift them as I have uplifted you. You and I, we shall go on to restore the glory lost in the dark hours of 1944. I feel his blood. It surges through me. His precious blood. You will help bring about this new glory, Klaus?"

"Ja," Gurnheim gasped, breathless. *"Ja, mein—"*

"No, not yet," "Durkey" said, smiling. Gurnheim wondered if Krieger's face ever did that.

2

"I've got a question for you, Major Track—"

Track raised his right hand, stopping the young Flying Squad sergeant. "Please, it's Mr. Track. I stopped being Major Track three years ago."

"That's what I wanted to ask, sir," the sergeant persisted. "Why did you leave the U.S. Army?"

Track leaned back against the chalk ledge of the blackboard, studying the eighteen faces he'd come to know in the past few days.

He looked down at the half-dozen different riot shotguns on the table in front of him: a Mossberg 500 ATP6P, Parkerized, Pro-Ported; an old High Standard 10B "Space Gun"; a 97 Winchester pump with exposed hammer; a modified Auto Five Browning; a Remington 870 with folding stock and extension magazine; and a black Franchi SPAS 12 with folding stock.

Track moved away from the blackboard and walked across the platform to lean against the table where the guns lay.

He sat on the edge, then began to speak. "I grew up in Chicago, south side. My parents were dead, and I lived with my older sister. I got into the gangs there. I joined to avoid getting beaten up. There was this gang of blacks. One of their members was killed in a rumble, and we all got hauled up before a judge. I was seventeen at the time and a high school dropout, a delinquent. Even though I didn't have a criminal record then, the judge said I'd pretty soon get one. So he gave me a couple of choices. The most attractive one was joining the military. Army was the only branch he could get to take me at seventeen with two years of high school. That was during the Vietnam War. They took anybody who could walk in those days.''

The Flying Squad members laughed. Track didn't.

"Instead of Vietnam, though, I wound up in West Germany. My first sergeant took a liking to me and encouraged me to get my G.E.D. That's General Educational Development or high school equivalency. All of a sudden I got interested in learning. By the time my first hitch was up, I was going to school and studying nights. I completed college in five years, and my first sergeant asked me if I wanted to become an officer. Well, I did.

"I kept going to school and stayed with CID. I was naturally good with weapons—always was. I specialized in tracking down gunrunners. Got involved in the whole terrorist thing. Then I figured maybe I could do more good as a civilian, teaching Special Weapons and Tactics.'' He shrugged, felt himself smile. "So, gentlemen, here I am.'' He looked down at his hands for a moment, then at the Flying Squad members. "Any other questions?''

The young sergeant raised his hand again.

Track nodded.

"Sir, what happened to the first sergeant—the one who sort of kept you under his wing, so to speak?''

Track cleared his throat. "There was a terrorist bombing—Baader Meinhof gang, we always figured. He—he died.'' Track forced his mouth into a smile.

"Now any questions? About these weapons, perhaps?"
He pointed to the table.

A voice called out from the back, "Corporal Simmons, sir!"

"Yes, Corporal?" Track nodded to the man, whose
hair seemed darker than the black coveralls he wore.

"Of all those shotguns you seemed to prefer the
SPAS. Could you tell us why, sir?"

Track nodded, picking up the SPAS. He released the
clip for the sling at the rear so he could fold out the
stock, snapping it out, then reclipping the sling just
above the stock hinge. He folded down the butt plate.
"It's personal preference largely. First of all, it's a
mean-looking sucker—and you need that. Who remembers what I said was one of the primary virtues of the
police shotgun?"

Several hands shot up, and Track picked a brown-
haired, slightly older corporal. "Go ahead."

"I believe you said, sir," the clipped voice came back,
"that the intimidation factor of the shotgun was one of
its more important aspects in police work."

Track snapped the shotgun up to his shoulder for an
instant, aiming toward the class. "Forgive the breach of
safe handling, but how many of you riveted your eyes
onto that muzzle for an instant?"

All hands raised.

"My point, gentlemen—meanness of the shotgun's
potential. But aside from the way it looks, semiautomatic functioning is faster for repeat shots. In pump
mode you can use these." Track reached to the table,
picking up a cylindrical black sabat. "What are these?"

The corporal with the jet-black hair raised his hand.
Track nodded.

"Sabats that allow firing either a .44 Magnum or a .38 Special or what-have-you out of a shotgun. They cycle just like a shotgun shell—made by a man named Trapper."

Track added, "They also eject just like one. They can be used for a variety of purposes, but the pump cycle allows added versatility. And what do you need in police weaponry?" He looked out to the men.

"Versatility," someone called out.

"Exactly. On the street you have to make do with the weapons at hand. The more you can do with them, the better off you are. It's simple logic." He set down the shotgun.

Suddenly an alarm sounded; the siren's wail grew in intensity. The men jumped from their seats at the sound of the voice over the loudspeaker. "This is not a drill. This is not a drill."

The eighteen men of the London Metropolitan Flying Squad were moving toward the polished brass firepole dominating the far right corner of the room. One after the other they dived toward it and disappeared below the circular hole in the floor.

Only one man beside Track still remained in the room—Inspector Hall, who was smiling oddly. "I say, Dan?"

"Yes?"

"Just a moment, will you?"

Track watched Hall walk across the room to the red wall-mounted telephone beside the chalkboard.

Hall picked up the receiver. "Central? Hall, here. What's the flap for the Flying Squad?" Hall nodded, looking thoughtful, his right thumb hooked into the right front pocket of the vest of his Oxford-gray suit. "Hmm, I see." He nodded again, extremely sober looking, Track thought. "At Marchand's—yes. How many?"

There was a pause. "And the bobby? Ethington—yes. Good chap. No—yes." Another long pause. "Cheerio," Hall said, and hung up.

Track looked at him.

"Nasty business, I'm afraid, Dan."

"What is it, Sir Edward?"

"IRA—that lot. They've taken over one of the top floors at Marchand's Department Store in the central business district. Ethington—Metropolitan man, known him for years. IDed them. Shot him dead through the chest. What you'd call a 'hit squad,' no doubt. Not sure how many hostages. They may have a bomb. Care to see the Flying Squad in action?"

Track raised his eyebrows. He looked at Hall, then reached for the SPAS, pocketing the .44 Magnum sabat. He felt under the table for the black nylon Safariland SWAT bag he carried his gear in.

Track started toward the firepole, slinging the SPAS diagonally cross-body under his right arm, shoving it back then across his back. He reached out to grasp the firepole; the SWAT bag's two fabric handles hung over his left wrist. He glanced back.

Sir Edward Hall was looking at him strangely. "My God, man, aren't you planning to use the stairs?"

Track smiled. "Always wanted to try one of these." Track threw himself out, wrapping his legs around the pole as he started to slide. His stomach lurched. It was faster down than he'd thought.

POLICE VANS AND CARS with flashing lights were everywhere. Firefighters stood near their gleaming trucks, hoses strung out along the streets and sidewalks. Track and Sir Edward Hall exited from a black Jaguar sedan.

The car was parked diagonally across the road from the main entrance to the store. The building seemed to occupy an entire city block; its brown stones and gray trim rose eighteen stories into the gray sky.

Track, the SPAS 12 slung from his left shoulder, followed Hall in a fast loping walk toward a knot of uniformed officers and plainclothesmen who were standing on the farthest side of the street from Marchand's.

He spotted a BBC television crew, their sound trucks back behind the police and fire lines.

Hall, slightly flushed, stopped at the center of the knot of police. Some of the men turned to him. A tall thin man with graying hair nodded, extending his hand. "Sir Edward, good to see you as always, sir."

"A hearty second to that, Bill," Hall murmured. Then Hall turned to Track, explaining, "Bill Tompkins is with the counterterrorist branch of the Home Office. Bill, this is Daniel Track, the Special Weapons expert I'd mentioned to you."

Track took Tompkins's outstretched hand.

"Mr. Track, I understand we share a mutual friend—Sir Abner Chesterton."

"The insurance man?"

Tompkins laughed. "I've heard Sir Abner called a good many things but never an insurance man."

"Still shilling for The Consortium, isn't he?"

"Yes," Tompkins replied. "I suppose if one looks at it that way, Sir Abner is an insurance man."

Track looked up toward the higher floors of the department store. "What's the story here?"

"Not very pretty, I'm afraid. Too many unknowns. Marchand's was running a heavily advertised sale in their ladies' foundations department. Could be any number of persons on the eighth floor—''

"Nine stories up, right," Track interrupted.

"By American reckoning, yes," Hall answered for Tompkins.

"We have evacuated all the floors above and below with the help of the fire-brigade chaps. But no telling how many are on the eighth floor. Anywhere from a dozen to a hundred or more. All elevators and stairwells are blocked. Our lads are on the rooftop." Track followed as Tompkins pointed out the positions of his men. "Every exit is blocked. Architectural plans for the building were on file in our offices, as they are for most edifices in the central business district." Tompkins smiled. "Been fighting these IRA bastards for quite some time. Like to be ready for them when they throw an unexpected soiree."

"How many in the IRA team?" Hall interrupted.

Tompkins turned around, tapping a tall thin policeman on the shoulder. The man saluted when he saw Hall. Tompkins said, "This is Carrington—first man on the scene when Ethington went down. Carrington, tell Sir Edward and this gentleman what you told me."

"Very well, sir," the young bobby began. "I reached Mr. Ethington at approximately eleven forty-seven. A chest wound seemed the most serious of the various wounds about his body."

More sirens were sounding; more police vans were pouring into the street from both directions. Track watched as their flak-jacketed occupants spilled out. "What kind of weapon would you say was used, Mr. Carrington?" Track interrupted.

"Automatic, I'd say, from the pattern of the wounds.

Looked to me like a small submachine gun, the kind that can be hidden under a coat. Close range, Ethington never had a chance, sir.''

"He gave you numbers?" Track asked, trying to remain dispassionate.

"Yes, sir. Five he saw, but there could have been more, sir. No mention of their arms. He recognized the leader, bloke named O'Malley. We've been wanting O'Malley for some time now."

"What say we go into the building and attempt to contact the terrorists. That's what they're waiting for, I presume," Sir Edward Hall suggested.

"How about if I go along? Maybe I can help."

"That's irregular," Tompkins chimed in.

"Yes. So irregular I don't have time to make a policy decision or consult with superiors." Hall smiled and turned to Track. "Come if you wish. Perhaps you can help."

Track picked up his black bag and adjusted the SPAS on its sling. "Ready when you are."

Hall nodded, starting forward, with Tompkins on his left and Track falling in on his right. Carrington, a sergeant, and the field commander for the Special Flying Squad, Theron Morgan, followed as the group entered the store. They stood next to the perfume counter, and Sir Edward Hall picked up the receiver of a telephone from a support-pillar-mounted cradle and began talking into it.

"This is Sir Edward Hall, Assistant Superintendent, Metropolitan Police, Scotland Yard. I'm addressing the men on the eighth floor. If you hear me, contact me using the telephone located near the foundation garments' dressing room. Dial three one six two and you'll reach me," he added, reading the typed number affixed to the cradle.

He hung up the phone. "We wait," he said, raising his eyebrows.

The telephone rang. Hall picked it up. "Yes, Sir Edward Hall here."

Track watched as Hall turned to Tompkins. "They have a list of demands." Tompkins nodded, taking out a pencil and notebook. Hall spoke into the receiver. "I'll be repeating what you say so it can be transcribed. Go ahead."

Track was becoming impatient. He clenched and unclenched his fists, then unzipped his brown leather bomber jacket, waiting.

"All police are to move six blocks away from the store—" Hall looked at Tompkins. "A bus to take you, along with some of the hostages, to Heathrow, and an aircraft to fly you to Libya." Hall cleared his throat. "And if we don't, what then?" Hall blanched, then seemed to turn gray. "I see. No, no need to repeat that. Yes, I'm certain I've got it. Yes, I'll call back." Hall hung up.

He took a gold watch out of his vest pocket and flicked open the case. He studied the watch a moment, then snapped the case shut, placing the watch in his pocket. "They claim," he sighed heavily, "to have a bomb and eighty-two hostages—women mostly, some children." He laughed. "They have a gay up there. I believe that's what you Americans call them?" Hall nodded to Track. "He was trying to buy a brassiere—for himself, apparently.

"At any rate, they claim they intend to detonate their bomb—a large one, fifteen sticks of dynamite—in exactly—'' he looked at his watch again ''—nine minutes and fifteen seconds if we don't begin to comply. One of the children is in a wheelchair. A little girl, O'Malley told me. And it was O'Malley.''

Track felt his jaw setting, the tendons in his neck going tight. His voice strained as he asked, ''This O'Malley—you figure he'd—''

''Detonate the bomb, killing eighty-two people, along with himself and his comrades?'' Tompkins broke in. ''Most assuredly.''

''He's just killed a bobby,'' Tompkins added. ''He's wanted for any number of crimes and acts of terrorism. It would be the end for him if he were taken alive. He knows that.''

Track sighed and picked up the SWAT bag, setting it on the perfume counter. He started to strip away his jacket. ''Anybody got a flak vest I can borrow? Nothing too heavy. I'll need to move around.''

''I say, Dan. This isn't . . . you can't—'' Hall started.

''I make a habit of picking only the best guys, the guys I'd work with if I had to. I need only these three men, Sir Edward.'' He nodded toward Carrington, the sergeant and Theron Morgan. ''Like you said, how much time is there to check with your superiors? I glanced at those plans.''

Track looked to his left at the architectural drawings for the store, which lay unrolled on the perfume counter. ''There's a utilities access shaft. I can take my three men up the shaft. You guys wait here. If I get shot up, you can always claim I went up without your knowledge. They can't be that eager to commit suicide that they wouldn't give you a second chance, maybe.''

From the Safariland bag he took a Cobra Com Match

shoulder rig and slipped it over his arms. Raising his arms over his head, he started to put it on, then stopped. "Almost forgot that flak vest," Track said, laughing.

Hall didn't laugh at all.

"THEY AREN'T MOVING out of the street yet," Coughlin, a ferret-faced man, reported to O'Malley. The man turned back to the floor-level window that was located at the exact corner of the triangular-shaped floor area. O'Malley was smiling.

"Didn't think they would now. That Sir Edward Hall—a tough bastard. Got Tompkins with him, too. The BBC down there watching it all. Didn't think they'd be after doin' it without a little proddin' now, hmm?"

O'Malley ran both hands across his face, pushing back the lock of brown hair that hung over his right eye. "Ah, better now, it is." He smiled, walking past the hostages. Some of the women were crying. One old woman had begged him not to make her kneel because her legs were stiff with arthritis. He made her kneel, anyway.

Only one person didn't kneel—the little girl in the wheelchair. She sat with her hands folded in the lap of her dress, looking up at him now.

He looked away from her, walking the line of hostages again, stopping in front of the homosexual. O'Malley had made him strip and kneel. He was naked except for the brassiere he'd been trying to buy. "How's it goin', faggy?"

The pale, thin-faced young man licked his lips. "I was going to a costume party. That's—that's—"

"Ah, and sure'n we know what kind of party it was, too, don't we now," O'Malley jeered, laughing.

He walked on, stopping beside the little girl in the wheelchair again. "Darlin', you're so pretty. 'Tis a shame for you to spend your whole little life in that there chair, it is. But I might fix that now." The little girl gazed up at him, her smile uncertain.

He looked at his four other men, then at Coughlin, beside the window; then at his wristwatch. Seven of the ten minutes were gone.

"Coughlin, take the butt of your pistol and knock the lock offn' that there winder. Open up the winder real high." He looked to his other four men, scattered beside the elevator bank, the stairwell and the fire escape. The one standing guard over the hostages was the one he selected. "Mick, be a good lad and help Coughlin. He's a mite skinny to work such a big winder now." O'Malley reached forward, placing his hands on the arms of the little girl's wheelchair. "Yes, darlin', 'tis a pity for you to live only half a life. Better no life at all."

The woman beside the wheelchair, to O'Malley's right, started to scream. O'Malley's right hand curled around the pistol grip of the MAC-11 .380 that hung from under his tweed sport coat as he leaned forward. He shoved the muzzle against the woman's forehead. He spoke to the woman. "Your burdens—they'll be lifted now, madam." The woman screamed again, reaching out for him with her hands, her nails bared. He smashed the pistol grip against her forehead, knocking her back.

The little girl screamed, "Mommie."

He shoved the MAC-11 against the tip of the little girl's nose. "Shh, darlin', hush now." He stood erect, watching the faces of the hostages. He liked the fear he saw there. He walked behind the wheelchair. His free hand grasped the left handle. He started to wheel the girl forward. As he passed the nearly naked young man, O'Malley heard someone move. He whirled as the homosexual attacked him, trying to wrestle the gun from him.

O'Malley kicked the man in the crotch. The man uttered a scream and slumped back. O'Malley fired a short burst into the man's face. His body thrashed, then lay still.

"Ya did have balls after all, boyo!" The IRA leader laughed, then pushed the wheelchair toward the open window, past the rest of the hostages, past the fifteen sticks of dynamite resting on a glass countertop.

"Gotta show those nasty policemen outside," he told the little girl, "that we mean business, darlin'. Don't we now?" The little girl was crying. O'Malley liked the way the air smelled fresher the closer he pushed her toward the open window.

TRACK CUPPED HIS RIGHT HAND over the face of the Rolex. In the semidarkness he was unable to read the luminous dial of the Sea Dweller, but now, under his hand, it was dark enough to see the time. Eight minutes had elapsed.

Track and the three men passed the stenciled numeral indicating the seventh floor. Ahead he could see the cracks of light for the access door to the eighth floor. He hoped that no one outside the service shaft could hear the sounds of movement.

Then Track heard Sir Edward Hall on the loudspeaker system, urging the terrorists to surrender. From his position in the shaft, the echoing words were hard to follow, but Track realized that Sir Edward was only trying to cover any telltale sounds Track, Theron Morgan and the two other men would make in reaching the eighth floor.

Track stopped climbing the ladder. His skin itched from the fiberglass insulation around him. His hands were sweating inside the black skintight leather gloves.

He looked down. Morgan and the two men were behind him.

Track shuffled the SPAS 12 forward with his left hand as he clung to the rungs with his right. The shotgun was wrapped in a fire-department blanket to prevent it banging against some metal object. Awkwardly he stripped away the blanket with his left hand.

The riot shotgun now hung pendulum fashion under his right arm. Under Track's left, over the flak vest, was one of two personal weapons he always carried. Nestled in the Cobra holster was an L-Frame stainless-steel Smith & Wesson revolver with a four-inch barrel. The Model 686 .357 Magnum had been customized by his friend Ron Mahoosky at Metalife Industries. The slab-sided barrel now carried Track's full name engraved on the right flat, and the letters were filled with gold. Action tuned, round butted—ready.

The noise of Sir Edward's speech over the PA system stopped abruptly.

With both hands grasping an overhead rung, Morgan swung back, then thrust himself forward. His feet came to rest noiselessly against the access doorframe. Track pushed Morgan from behind to give the Flying Squad leader a better balance on the access doorframe.

Track nodded to Theron Morgan, and Morgan twist-

ed the handle of the access door, swinging the door
slightly open.

In the semidarkness of the shaft, there was a pale
wash of yellow light now from the opening in the access
doorway. Track could see Morgan raise one finger.
Track understood—one terrorist visible from the door.

Track reached over to the grab handle, pulling himself across the open space of the shaft. Crouching, he
pushed gently on the door. Hugging the black SPAS 12
against his body, he went through the doorway. Track
heard a faint rustle as Morgan started to follow him. He
squinted against the sudden brightness of the floor's
lights.

The man Morgan had indicated was now beside the
drinking fountain near the elevator bank, his head
turned away from the access shaft.

Morgan started to reach for the silenced 7.65mm
Walther PP that he wore in a shoulder holster.

Track stayed Morgan's hand, shaking his head. Then
Track reached for his own belt instead.

His right hand found the borrowed Gerber MK II
fighting knife. He slowly opened the snap on the safety
strap and clamped the double-edged blade between his
teeth. He started forward in a long-strided crouch. He
had covered half the distance to the man beside the
drinking fountain when he heard a woman scream.
Track froze.

Then an Irish-accented male voice said, "The darlin'
girl won't feel much of a thing. Her legs are paralyzed,
anyway, now aren't they?"

Track saw the guard tense.

"Damn," Track rasped under his breath, taking off
in a silent run toward the guard. The man seemed to

sense something. He glanced over his right shoulder, then turned. Track's right hand flashed forward. His gloved left hand clamped over the guard's mouth and nose while the right plunged the Gerber into the terrorist's right kidney. Drawing out the spear-point blade, Track jabbed it into the man's throat, cutting the voice box.

Track left the knife in place and caught the body as it slumped toward him. He flattened himself in a corner against the wall, moving the SPAS 12 forward.

The Irish voice began again—Track was certain it was O'Malley. "And what's the matter with you, Terrence? No stomach to watch a pretty little girl go for a flight in the air?"

Track wondered if the dead guard was Terrence.

Track heard the sound of a whimper, then the woman screamed again, "Don't push my baby out the window!"

"For the good of the cause, madam. For the good of the cause, it is!"

Track had the first finger of his right hand into the trigger guard; the right-side safety level was already set to the firing position. The trigger-guard safety edged forward as his trigger finger pressed against it.

The first round up was two-and-three-quarter-inch high-brass double O buck. Track looked at Morgan and nodded once.

"Now!" Track shouted as he hurled himself around the corner, dashing past the elevator bank. The scene that appeared before him was like a tableau.

A man, brown hair down to his collar and across his forehead, was standing beside an open window. The windowsill was at floor level. A young girl sat in a wheelchair, covering her eyes with her hands. The man was about to push the wheelchair out the window.

Track shouted, "O'Malley, no!"

A red-haired man was turning toward him, raising his SMG to fire. Track pumped the trigger of the SPAS 12, hitting the man with the full shot load. The volley of double O buck picked up the redhead, hurling him back against an eight-foot-high glass display cabinet. The body smashed into the glass, shattering it. Headless mannequin torsos wearing bras and girdles tumbled around the dead man. Track triggered the SPAS again. The alternating slug load tore off the left arm of the ferret-faced man, who was standing beside O'Malley and the little girl.

O'Malley thrust the wheelchair forward out the window. Track saw the chair and its occupant hang there for an instant. Then they disappeared. The girl's shriek was lost in the pandemonium. The terrorist leader began to turn, bringing up a submachine gun.

To his right, Track saw the ferret-faced man—the stump that was his left arm gushing blood—lurching toward an electrical detonator near a taped pile of dynamite sticks.

Track jabbed the muzzle of the riot shotgun against the man's body. Blood and flesh exploded in a crimson mist as he pulled the trigger. The terrorist's body fell toward him.

Track started to fall as O'Malley's subgun began to chatter. He twisted his head and neck free of the riot shotgun's web sling. With his right hand he drew out one of the stainless-steel *shuriken* throwing spikes from the back of his left glove. He drew back his right arm, then flicked his wrist forward, hurling the *shuriken* toward O'Malley.

O'Malley's body spun as his left hand reached up, tugging at the spike embedded in his chest. His subgun sprayed harmlessly into the floor. Track's right hand found the butt of the Metalife Custom L-Frame, whipping it out of the Cobra rig. His left hand came up to brace his right in police position as he pumped the trigger. The stainless .357 Magnum bucked three times. O'Malley's body twitched each time. Track fired again and again until the six rounds were gone.

O'Malley weaved, refusing to go down; the subgun still rose. Track ran toward O'Malley, then planted his right foot as he half wheeled. His left leg snapped up and out, impacting on O'Malley's throat.

"Damn you, boyo!" O'Malley croaked. His body tumbled backward and his head and shoulders grazed the wooden window frame. O'Malley's body then flew through the window as the subgun fired into the ceiling.

Chunks of plaster rained down on Track. The gunfire around him stopped.

Track looked behind him once. Morgan stood there, a Sterling subgun in his hand. The other two Flying Squad men were there, too. No one was wounded. Some of the women and children were crying.

The IRA men and the homosexual lay dead on the floor.

Then Track heard it—a small voice coming from outside the window. "Help me, please...."

Track raced to the window. He put down the gun in the broken glass and blood and leaned out over the floor-level sill.

There were knots of men on the street standing around what looked like a twisted mass of wheels and tubing. Others stood around something that could have been a body.

Firemen were running out with a net.

Track looked slightly to his right.

Halfway down the floor below dangled the little girl, part of her dress caught on the point of a flagpole. Her hands were grasping a ripping Union Jack.

"Jesus," Track rasped. He looked behind him. "Morgan, get my shotgun. Hurry!"

Track stripped off the shoulder rig and the flak vest, throwing both down behind him.

He pulled his trouser belt from the loops of his Levi's.

Morgan returned with the SPAS 12. "Here, Major."

Track snatched the shotgun. He unhooked the clips of the front and rear sling swivels, working the sling's buckle to open the sling out completely. He hooked both clips through the solid-brass buckle of the black Safariland belt. "Hold this," he rasped to Morgan. "Don't let go, or you'll lose us both." Track slipped the sling over his head and shoulders, settling it under his armpits.

Morgan wrapped the tongue of the belt around his fist. "This won't hold you, sir!"

"Damn well better," Track snapped, stepping out onto the ledge.

"Hurry up, please!" whimpered the little girl.

Track looked down at her. "Hold on, honey. You'll be fine. Just hold that flag and don't move!" he coaxed the handicapped girl.

Track looked back to see Morgan out on the ledge behind him. Morgan's right hand was locked into a clamp for the window washer.

"Now if you didn't like my small-arms course," Track began, placing his knees at the edge of the twelve-inch-wide ledge, "letting go of that belt isn't the way to tell me about it." Track eased his hands to the ledge, letting down one knee, then the other. His right foot rested on the base of the flagpole when he extended the toe of his shoe.

Track lowered himself slowly. All that held him now were Morgan, the belt and the sling from the SPAS 12.

Track straddled the flagpole. He could feel the pole pressing into his testicles. He glanced up to Morgan. "Test this for me. Let out some slack on your end of the harness—just a little." He felt the easing tension where the sling bound against his armpits, then felt the pole sag slightly, but it held. "Now I'm going out to get her. Hang in there, Morgan," Track shouted over the police sirens below.

Track stretched forward, and his gloved hands eased across the length of the flagpole. At his longest reach the little girl was still more than two feet away. He leaned his weight out to full extension along the pole as his knees gripped it tightly. The pole sagged more under him.

Moving his knees millimeters at a time, he edged forward. The little girl was crying for her mother.

He inched forward slowly again, feeling the pole bending some more under their combined weight.

Once more he reached out. Then he had her. He gripped her left hand.

"Gotcha, honey!" he shouted at her.

He tried pulling her up, but her dress was still caught in the point of the flagpole. The pole that had saved her life now endangered it. The flagpole swayed and creaked as the wind gusted.

"Hell," Track rasped.

The little girl's eyes widened as she looked up at him. She said, crying, "Mommie told me that's a bad word."

"Mommie's right." He nodded, trying to distract the girl from her predicament.

Breathless, Track thought desperately of a way to un-snag her dress. Then he had it. He reached his free hand down, pulling another *shuriken* spike from the back of the left glove. The *shuriken* was identical to the one he'd thrown into O'Malley's chest.

He stabbed the point of the spike into the fabric of the dress, punching the tiny blade through half its length, ripping at the material. He tugged harder. The material around the collar was stronger—but it ripped, too. Track freed the girl, feeling her full weight—fifty or sixty pounds, he judged—in his right hand.

He tossed the *shuriken* back toward the building, hoping it didn't land on anyone below.

Track looked at the little girl. His right hand clung to what was left of her dress, and his fingers were knotted into her hair. "This'll hurt, sweetheart, but I have to do it."

The little girl screamed as he pulled her up.

Track shifted his body weight so he wouldn't slip off the pole. "Now," he gasped, swallowing hard, "get on my back. Knot your fingers into my clothes in front and hug my neck. Can you do that?"

She was already doing it; Track could feel her weight on him. He also felt her hands around his neck, tugging at his snap-fronted blue cowboy shirt. He started to edge his body back along the flagpole's length. He kept moving. The flagpole creaked under their weight now.

"Keep coming, Major!" It was Morgan's voice.

Track nodded, licking his dry lips, edging back farther. His hands were damp in the gloves.

Then his right foot felt something hard. He twisted

slightly, almost losing his balance. His fingers locked tighter onto the flagpole. His right foot was against the side of the building.

He kept moving backward, and his left foot made contact now.

"Morgan, vacation's over. Start pulling when I say go!"

"Yes, sir!"

His hands pushed against the flagpole; his feet were planted against the building.

"Now all you got," and he pushed his arms out to maximum extension. The sling for the SPAS 12 hurt as the tension increased across his chest. He reached his arms behind him when they could no longer do him any good, getting the girl tighter against him as he leaned back.

"Grab the little girl," he gasped, standing now, extending his right hand up to the ledge. He looked behind him and saw Morgan taking her up; the sling stayed taut.

He reached across his body with his left hand to touch the ledge.

"Got her, sir, inside and safe."

Track said nothing, just let Morgan haul him up. He pushed with his feet, sprawling half across the ledge. Morgan's hands were on him, helping to untie the sling. Then Track half crawled through the smashed window into the foundations department.

He sat back on a small chair one of the hostages moved out for him. "Thanks, lady," he said as he watched the little girl being cuddled in her mother's arms.

3

George Beegh shifted the Colt Combat Government .45 on his right hip to a better position, leaned back in the truck cab and tried to close his eyes. Just then the truck hit a bump, and the rig bounced. "Hell, Marvin, I'm trying to sleep."

"Relax, George, just relax."

"I'm trying to relax, Marvin. Just stop hitting every damn pothole in the road."

"Whole road's a pothole, man," Marvin snapped.

George cocked back the peak of his black Jack Daniels baseball cap, then turned to look at Marvin Lundy. He didn't say anything but kept watching Marvin, who looked as if he wanted to talk. George shrugged and stared at the windshield wipers moving back and forth.

"This damned rain," Marvin remarked.

George still watched the windshield wipers.

"When I signed on to drive nuclear shipments I never figured it'd be like this."

George closed his eyes. "I figured it'd be like this," George answered without being asked.

"How long were you in the Air Force, George?"

"Six years."

"That intelligence stuff you did—couldn't you get yourself a better job than this?"

George thought about that for a moment, then pulled his hat down over his eyes. "Yeah, but I figured for a few years I'd travel around, see the country. Good a way as any."

"Good a way as any," Marvin repeated, sneering.

Lightning flashed across the narrow two-lane blacktop, illuminating everything on the other side of the windshield for a moment.

"See, you and me, we're different," Marvin continued. "I've been doing this for three years now. You been at it less than a year, George."

"So what?"

"You get tired driving along in funny McDonald's trucks or hauling a half of a double wall like this thing." Marvin jabbed his thumb in the semidarkness toward the rear of the cab and the half of a huge mobile home in tow—it was fourteen feet wide.

George turned his attention from the windshield wipers to the pilot car ahead of them with the yellow flashers on its roof. They made far less light than the lightning as it ripped across the sky.

"Hauling nuclear material is hauling nuclear material, Marvin. It doesn't matter what the cover rig looks like," George said.

"This isn't nuclear material and you know it."

"What do you call nuclear warheads?" George asked him.

"Oh, yeah. I mean it's nuclear and all that, but those warheads are armed."

"No, they aren't," George told him, feeling disgusted.

"Well, next best thing. The detonators aren't reliable. That electrical storm three days ago almost blew one up in the silo."

"The trailer's insulated against electrical discharge. They put special insulating material around the warheads in the silos. Nothing can go wrong. The R-43 is a good system. Least it was until this kinky stuff came up."

"One hundred of those suckers."

"Yeah, but we'll only be hauling twenty-five of them. They've got three other teams out."

"What the hell guarantee have we got, George, that this insulation'll stop it? What if a lightning bolt hits the double wall back there?"

George watched the way Marvin was looking at him instead of the road. "What if you drive this rig off the side of the road and we go over the cliff there. Wise up, Marvin. Relax, huh?"

Marvin always did that to him. When it was George's turn to drive, Marvin slept like a rock, and when Marvin was driving, he talked, so George couldn't sleep.

"Hell," he snarled, trying to roll over. The butt of his gun dug into his ribs, but he had to carry it. He smiled at the thought. Almost nobody in the real world was "licensed to kill." He'd been six years in Air Force intelligence, part of the time overseas, and he'd never even carried a gun. But if you worked a team on a nuclear-transport truck, you had to carry a gun. You were told to shoot first and ask questions afterward if you had any doubts in the situation.

Plutonium was what they usually hauled. What terrorists could do with stolen plutonium was too horrible even to consider.

What they could do with the twenty-five defective nuclear warheads he and Marvin would be hauling—or the seventy-five others that three other rigs would be hauling—was even more horrible.

"Dammit," he said, and sat up. He couldn't sleep.

GEORGE WAS AT THE WHEEL; the truck was stopped. Rain was pelting down now with such force he could see the raindrops bounce off the Peterbilt's hood. Between the moving windshield wipers he watched the two air policemen who drove the pilot car with the flashers on it. They were standing in the rain, talking with the guards at the gate.

"Hurry up, guys," he sighed impatiently. While the cargo was being loaded he could grab some coffee and something to eat. And maybe get some sleep.

The two air policemen turned away from the gate guards and got back into their car. The guards wore yellow slickers and Stetsons, and were ostensibly cowboys guarding the entrance to a ranch, because the missile sites themselves were secret. One of the guards opened the gate; it swung inward. George started through the gate, easing out the clutch as he shifted out of neutral. Beside him, Marvin slept like a baby.

GEORGE HAD EATEN three microwaved hamburgers and drunk more coffee than he knew was good for him. He stood in the "barn" door now, his Jack Daniels cap pulled low over his face. The interior of the barn led to the missile-silo complexes themselves. The rain was still pouring down. He lit a Winston and stared out at the rain, then turned back toward the barn.

The side wall to the left of the barn doors was partially removed and there, barely under the loft, was parked the rear end of the rig. In the shelter of the barn men wearing Air Force fatigues with revolvers on their hips worked with forklifts. They were loading wooden containers onto the truck.

George knew the containers were heavily insulated. The detonation and actual warhead elements of the missiles were wrapped inside the insulation. They were parts of a multiple reentry vehicle system. Each warhead kilotonnage was in the five hundred range. That was all he'd been told.

"Twenty-five times five hundred," he murmured. Twelve thousand five hundred kilotons—it translated to twelve and one half megatons of thermonuclear destruction in back of his truck cab.

He shrugged under his brown corduroy vest. He wiggled his toes in his cowboy boots, staring at the tips for a moment. Then he straightened himself, feeling the rubbing of the Colt Combat Government in the Bianchi rig on his right hip.

He was beginning to think Marvin was right—there had to be better jobs.

4

Gurnheim sat staring down at the open shackles between his legs, tossing the keys in the air, then catching them again. He was listening to Johannes Krieger whistling a tune; the pleasant sounds came from the open bathroom door. Gurnheim wondered what Krieger really looked like but supposed he was better off not knowing.

"Johannes?"

"Yes?" the voice called back.

"Why did you need me? There are others who can plant bombs. You do it well. I should know—" he laughed "—I taught you."

They were in a small house located in a rural area of Hamburg. The house was evidently lived in—there wasn't so much as a speck of dust on the coffee table beside which he sat. He turned his attention now from the shackles to the fireplace. A fire had been burning when they arrived. The sedan they had driven had been abandoned on a side road four miles or so back and the two dead policemen rolled out into a ditch.

Gurnheim looked toward the bathroom as he heard footsteps. "Krieger?"

The figure that greeted him now was not that of Durkey, the British police inspector, but rather an attractive, dark-haired woman dressed as an airline stewardess. Other than the height—and the three-inch heels helped that—the disguise was perfect... feminine, beautiful. "What's this?"

"Call it an economical way of traveling without my luggage being fluoroscoped, without having to pass my body through a metal detector."

Then the voice changed, rising half an octave but not sounding at all strained or faked. Gurnheim felt embarrassed thinking it, but the voice sounded like that of his deceased mother.

"Coffee, tea, or—" Then the voice changed back. Krieger laughed. He walked across the room and sat at the far end of the couch, his skirt pulled demurely over his knees. He brushed an auburn curl back from his forehead. As he talked, he opened the purse that was on his lap. The combination of masculine voice and feminine appearance was almost too much for Gurnheim to concentrate on what Krieger was saying.

"My dear Klaus, you are a specialist. You are terrible at assassinations, clumsy with a knife. That policeman you killed just before you were captured—how awkward. You are worse still with a gun." Krieger touched up his lipstick in a compact mirror. "But you are a genius with explosives. And I will give you the ultimate explosive, the ultimate challenge. When you get to America, of course."

"I do not understand. I have never been to America."

"A beautiful country. The people are ridiculously friendly and trusting, the scenery in some places more beautiful than one can imagine. And anyway, our explosives are there."

"What kind of explosives?"

Krieger ignored the question, closing his purse. He

stood up, smoothing the skirt down along his thighs as he walked to the bar.

Gurnheim noticed his hands—the nails were long and painted pink.

"Do you go to the movies?"

"Yes, I like the movies, Johannes."

"I studied long and hard to be an actor. I played in some films. In one I played a henchman to a supervillain fighting a superspy—the kind who always gets to make love to the incredibly beautiful woman at the end of the film. You know the kind of movie, yes?"

"Yes," Gurnheim replied, taking a cigarette from a box on the coffee table and lighting it.

Krieger was pouring himself a glass of sparkling wine. "A drink, Klaus?"

"No, not now."

"Champagne goes with the role I play," Krieger explained, sipping at the wine. "In America, by the way, they use flat glasses for champagne—boorish."

Gurnheim watched him, just then noticing the proper champagne glass—tulip shaped—that Krieger drank his wine from. "But—"

"I need you to help me reverse that superspy supervillain image, Klaus. The villain always wants to dominate the world for some sinister purpose." Krieger walked around the bar, easing himself up onto a bar stool, crossing his shaven legs.

The legs were good looking, Gurnheim thought.

"One could say I'm a villain. At least by conventional standards I certainly am. And I do plan to dominate the world." Krieger stirred his champagne until it fizzed, using his left index finger. He sucked the champagne from his finger.

"Stop it, Johannes!"

Krieger laughed, sliding down from the bar stool. "Old friend, to play a role one must live a role."

"I do not understand this world domination, this—"

"You will help me—so that I may actually irrevocably rule the world, create the new order we both serve. That's all I can say now. Will you help me, Klaus, as only you can?"

Gurnheim studied Krieger's eyes. They were icy blue, and he assumed Krieger was wearing contact lenses. They were a little insane, too, he thought. But he nodded. "Yes, yes, Johannes. I will help you—in this thing, in all things."

The graceful right hand reached out to him; the champagne glass was set down.

Gurnheim took the hand. The grip was more powerful than a vise.

"Good," Krieger said in his own voice. Then in his feminine voice he whispered, "Such a dear man you are, Klaus." And he laughed.

5

Sir Abner Chesterton was having difficulty adjusting his lap belt. The auburn-haired, blue-eyed stewardess leaned down as she passed him. She was very tall, and he liked tall women.

"May I help you with that, Sir Abner?"

"Yes. Yes, you may," he said, smiling up at her.

The woman brushed back a lock of hair with a pink manicured fingernail and returned a smile. "Let me raise your table for you," she offered again.

"You're a lovely girl," Chesterton told her, feeling rather silly saying this, but powerless not to.

She smiled, a warm pretty smile, inviting. "Thank you very much, sir." Then she reached down and gave a final tug to his lap belt.

"What's your name?" He'd never asked a stewardess her name before.

"Johanna, sir. Are you comfortable now? We'll be landing at Heathrow in about five minutes according to the captain."

"Yes, very comfortable, Johanna." He smiled at her.

They were stacked over Heathrow Airport, awaiting clearance to land. Johanna came back and sat in the empty seat beside him. "I understand you're an insurance investigator," she said, looking into his eyes.

He could feel her piercing gaze. "It sounds like such an interesting profession."

"I imagine men must say that to you constantly—as a flight attendant."

She smiled, nodding only slightly, still looking at him.

"It's really rather a dull job, I confess. I represent a cartel of some of the largest transglobal underwriters. We call ourselves The Consortium. I'd venture to say one of our member companies insures you, insures this aircraft, perhaps even Heathrow Airport."

"But a titled man an insurance investigator?"

"A hereditary title, I'm afraid. My grandfather was a young man when he saved Queen Victoria's life. She was so grateful she made him a knight and decreed that each succeeding eldest son retain the honor." Chesterton laughed apologetically. "Not like in the storybooks, I'm afraid, running around in armor and jousting for the attentions of fair damsels—like you, if you don't mind my saying so."

She only smiled.

He decided she didn't mind the comparison.

"But what do you do, then?" she asked, taking a cigarette from the pocket of her skirt. "We're not supposed to smoke in front of the passengers, but then I do so hate being stacked."

"The no-smoking sign is off at any rate, my dear," and he produced his gold Dunhill and flicked it, lighting her cigarette, then lighting one for himself.

"But what do you do?" she repeated, exhaling a long thin stream of smoke through her pursed lips.

"I work with Interpol and various European and American police agencies—like Scotland Yard, the Sûreté, the FBI. We pursue terrorists."

"That must be very dangerous," Johanna commented.

"Hardly," he laughed, feeling happy, expansive. If there hadn't been the dinner appointment with Dan Track, he would have dared ask her out. But he wondered if he would have. "All I do is coordinate the flow of information. These bloody terrorists—excuse my language, my dear—have eyes and ears everywhere. And in the final analysis, when the wreckage is sifted through, the bodies counted, it's the insurance companies who pay. Dearly. And then all of us pay, of course. Our premium rates go up. We're talking potential billions in losses as terrorism spreads."

She shuddered, her shoulders shaking. "Are you cold, my dear?"

"No, but the thought of people doing such horrible things. I guess it makes me afraid." She smiled, looking up at him.

He licked his lips. "I say, er, Johanna. Do you, I mean, well, perhaps I shouldn't ask or mention this—no, I shouldn't."

"I can't tonight, Sir Abner."

"Well, actually, I can't, either. But I suppose it's always the same for you...I mean, suitors hovering about and all...a girl like you."

She seemed to laugh—perhaps a private joke, but he never thought she was laughing at him. "Some other time," she said, looking down at her hands folded in the lap of her skirt.

He licked his lips again. "Yes, I'd like that very much, Johanna."

"Do you have a card? I could give you my phone number."

"Yes, certainly." He searched the pockets of his vest for his card case, found it. He also extracted a gold Cross pen from his pocket, twisting the point out, handing both pen and card to her.

"It's just an answering service. I share it with some of the other girls," she said as she wrote down the number. He took the card and the pen from her. The handwriting was spidery thin, unmistakably feminine. He produced another card, handing it to her.

"My number, if you, er, ever need. . . ."

Her left hand reached out, rested for the briefest instant over his right. The No Smoking sign dinged, and she stood, extinguishing the cigarette, lipstick on the filter tip, as he watched her. "I won't forget," she promised as she edged past him.

He felt silly for saying it. "Neither will I." He watched her walk down the aisle away from him.

"I SAY, TRACK, how often is it that I talk with you?"

"About once every two months or so."

"How many times have I bought you dinner only to have you refuse working for The Consortium?"

"Counting this time?" Track smiled, sipping at his drink—a double Seagrams Seven, ice cubes and a splash of water. Chesterton thought the concoction was repulsive. "This makes eight times."

"Dammit, Track, this whole bloody terrorist business is serious—like the affair yesterday at Marchand's."

"You make it up into the foundations department much?"

"Don't be bloody funny, Track. I'm really serious."

Sir Abner watched him smile. Track's gray eyes were

laughing, and his dark brown hair reminded him of the stewardess. He shook his head to clear it.

"I'm not really trying to be funny, Sir Abner. I'm really flattered that The Consortium thinks I could be such a big help. But I'm not interested." He set down his drink. "Now you can wine me and dine me in another sixty days or so—I'll never pass up a free meal—but the answer'll be the same, Sir Abner."

"But your qualifications, man—they are needed in the fight."

"Bullshit," Track told him calmly.

"Bullshit, indeed, sir. Fourteen years—"

"Almost fifteen."

"Quite. Fifteen years in the Army. Three years in Japan, two in Saigon—Fourth degree black belt in karate—"

"Tae Kwon Doe, actually."

"Very well, Tae Kwon Doe. A ranking combat shooter, expert with all types of firearms—"

"I grew up in a bad neighborhood. It left me with feelings of insecurity."

"Good God, there's no man as skilled with weapons as you are—knives, guns, martial-arts training, fifteen years in the U.S. Army Criminal Investigation Division tracking down terrorists and smugglers."

"Got boring," Track said, opening a black leather case and taking a thin cigar made of very dark tobacco from it. He rested the case on the table, then clipped the end of the cigar with a tiny guillotine. He lit the cigar with a Zippo lighter.

"This wouldn't be boring," Chesterton said, leaning back.

"I'm sure it wouldn't," Track agreed. "But I'm not

bored with what I do now. I travel all over the world. I teach weapons, officer survival, unarmed combat techniques. I write articles, a few books. I make a good living. I've got a little place in New Mexico—on time with the mortgage payments and everything. What's wrong with the life I live?''

"What's wrong with doing the same thing you did yesterday, but for us?"

Track smiled, exhaling a cloud of gray smoke from the cigar. "You mean play guns with terrorists?"

"My God, Track, those cigars. Each time I see you I wonder how you can smoke them. Yes, not just playing guns, but tracking them down."

"I get involved in the shooting end of things very little these days. You know that," Track explained.

"Don't you see, your name really says it all. We need you—as Dan Track, but also to track for us—track the terrorists and stop them."

Track laughed. "Track? You've been reading too many thriller novels, watching too many movies."

Chesterton sat bolt upright, took a swallow of his Scotch and water, then said, "The international terrorists have a network, an organization. We have cooperating police departments. We have Interpol, which isn't an enforcement agency at all, as you well know. We have the various intelligence organizations, but they never tell all they know. We need one man, a man we can send in wherever it is to track these bloody bastards down and kill them."

Track smiled.

"You could stick to your profession, use it as a cover," Sir Abner continued.

Track sat up, putting the cigar down in a glass ashtray

near his right hand. "I hope you find somebody. If I think of a name or something tomorrow on the way back to Albuquerque, I'll let you know. I've got classes to teach, some articles to finish, some guns to test. And Dorothy needs me."

"Dorothy?"

"That's right. You've never been to my place up in the mountains between Albuquerque and Sante Fe."

"Who's Dorothy?"

"I never told you about Dorothy?" Track started to feel around in his pockets, producing a leather wallet. He opened it, putting down his driver's license, concealed-weapons carry permits, insurance and credit cards beside his plate. He finally selected a photograph. Smiling, he seemed to study the photograph. Then he turned it over, making it right side up as he handed it across the small centerpiece to Chesterton.

Chesterton looked at Track, then at the photograph.

"A bloody cat?"

"No," he said defensively. "She's a tabby."

"Dorothy?"

"Dorothy The Wonder Cat."

"What?" Chesterton looked at the photograph again. A cat looking half asleep, half bored, sitting on top of a folded newspaper on what appeared to be a kitchen countertop. "Why do you call her The Wonder Cat?"

"It's a wonder that I keep her."

TRACK STOOD under the steaming hot shower. He had washed his hair twice, conditioned it once. Now his hands were lathering soap over his body. He shook his head, laughing. "Chesterton, what a—" But he didn't finish what he started to say.

Terrorism was out of control, and that was obvious to anyone, Track realized.

Chesterton had told him that of the eighty-odd people who had been hostages at Marchand's, forty-six of them had carried life insurance with one or more members of The Consortium. The store itself was insured against loss by one of the members of The Consortium, as were several of the buildings in the immediate vicinity of Marchand's, buildings that would have been damaged had the dynamite been exploded.

One incident and millions of dollars could have been lost. The loss in human lives would have gone beyond any dollar value.

Chesterton had said it was one of the rare instances where cold-blooded business sense and humanistic altruism both had the same goal. Stop the terrorists—as many and as often as possible. Save lives and vast sums of money.

Track set the soap down, bending his head into the shower spray, rinsing the conditioner from his hair. He let the hard spray pelt his body. Then he turned the water straight cold.

He glanced at the Rolex on his left wrist. It was almost 5:30 A.M. He had been up with Chesterton until one, then slept until five. His plane would be leaving Heathrow at seven-forty. He could sleep on the plane, he told himself. Getting his guns through customs always took a long time even though the paperwork on them was always in order. He smiled, thinking it was likely that customs men enjoyed seeing guns—which was why they took so long inspecting them.

He turned his face up toward the cold water. He was flying on the same airline Chesterton had flown out of Germany. Maybe he'd meet that same auburn-haired stewardess Chesterton had raved about on and off all evening.

"Johanna," he said.

He laughed at himself. He said another name—a name he had greater interest in.

"Desiree Goth."

6

The car had stopped; its ignition was off. He was getting to detest cars. It would feel good to blow up some again.

He heard the crunching footsteps on the gravel as he squinted at the darkness rimming the glare of the yellow headlights. He turned to the driver beside him. "Get out here?"

"Yes, here," said the dark mustached little man, nodding in the semidarkness. The only illumination in the car was the greenish glow from the gauges on the Volvo's dashboard.

"Here," Gurnheim said, then worked the door handle, opening it, stepping out.

Someone spoke from the far edge of the lights. A body was partially visible; hands held a submachine gun. "Welcome to Ankara, Herr Gurnheim," the voice said in English, the Turkish accent thick.

"A little bird told me cuckoo," Gurnheim said lifelessly.

"But only on the hour," the voice came back.

Gurnheim hated passwords—they were always stupid sounding. "Why does a Gray Wolf carry a Jew-made submachine gun?"

"It works well," came the voice from beyond the headlights. Then the body stepped fully into the glare, sporting an Uzi hanging from its sling. The man lit a cigarette with a match that made a whooshing sound as it flared. The acrid smell of phosphorous stung Gurnheim's nostrils.

"It does, I guess. Where to from here?" Gurnheim queried.

"Two hours from now, a plane will fly you to Madrid with two stopovers. I have your travel papers. They aren't that good, but they will get you to Madrid. In Madrid you will be given new papers. They will be very good. Then to America. I don't know what your name will be, Herr Gurnheim."

"So long as they don't make me sound like a Jew."

The Turk said nothing, only smoked his cigarette.

7

George Beegh reached behind the cab seat to where the gear was stored. Marvin Lundy was driving again. A second tractor trailer had joined them with its pilot car. They were transporting two loads of warheads—twenty-five megatons in all between them.

George was trying not to let it make him nervous. He had driven half the night; the other half he had been kept awake by Marvin's incessant griping and chattering.

He wondered what the other two loads of missile warheads were disguised as. Though the morning sky was not that bright—it was gray and overcast—he was too jumpy, too hyper to sleep.

He found his stuff sack and confirmed that it was his—Marvin's bag was identical—by the luggage tag on the handle. He opened the bag, digging inside.

There were two paperback novels. He settled on one he had read before, a story by the French philosopher Camus, then zipped his bag closed and turned around in the seat beside Marvin.

"What are you reading, George?"

"Camus."

"That French fella?"

"Yeah, that French fella."

"Hey, you want something good? I've got this illustrated novel I picked up in the truck stop. The one with all the funny stuff?''

"No, thanks. I'm just looking to read something light.''

"Right,'' Marvin said after a moment. "Well, if you want something good, just turn yourself around and grab my bag. The book's right on top under the catalog.''

"Catalog?''

"Got it the same place I got the book. They run a mail-order business in novelties and such.''

"Oh,'' George said, going back to his book.

"Hey, George?''

George looked up from the book over at Marvin Lundy. "What, Marvin?''

"I was thinking.''

"Yeah?''

"About what we were talking about the other night, last night?''

"What—what were—''

"That this job ain't so bad. I guess you're right.''

"Why?'' George asked him.

"See that newspaper I picked up last night?''

"No.''

"Here.'' Marvin leaned down with his left arm, pulling a rolled up newspaper out of the map pocket on the side of the driver's door.

George opened it up. The headlines read, "Train Carrying Nuclear Warheads Mobbed by Demonstrators.''

"No, sir,'' Marvin said after a moment, his voice lower, thoughtful sounding. "Wouldn't want to be riding that decoy train.''

George folded the paper and went back to Camus.

8

Miles Jefferson leaned closer to the small mirror, studying his face. His milk-chocolate-colored skin had always been large pored, and he had an ingrown hair. He picked at it with the tweezers from his Dopp kit, getting the root and grunting as he tugged it free.

He replaced the tweezers, studying his left cheek carefully for a minute. "Damn," he murmured, then put the Dopp kit on the lip of the sink.

He depressed the foot pedal, cupping the cold water that came out of the single spigot into his large spatulate-fingered hands. He splashed the water on his face.

Jefferson was tired.

He found a towel and rubbed it across his face, closing his eyes, then opening them. "Didn't do a bit of good," he commented to the mirror.

He hung the towel and turned away from the sink, picking up the Dopp kit. Then he opened the door of the closet-size bathroom and stepped out into the caboose proper.

As special agent in charge of the detail guarding the train, he was allowed to share the caboose with the railroad conductor. It was better than a sleeping bag in a boxcar like his men. But there was still no shower, and the bed was short for his frame.

Jefferson was a tall man—six foot five. When he'd played basketball in college, everyone had told him height was an advantage. He smiled at the thought; it was evident that "everyone" had never slept in a bunk aboard a rocking caboose.

He found his three-inch blue Model 13 Smith .357— the issue gun—and took it out of the little Alessi inside the pants holster. He broke the cylinder and loaded six 158-grain lead hollowpoint .38 Specials into the gun. He closed the cylinder and returned the gun to the leather, then settled the holster behind his right hip near his kidney, at the hollow of his back. He used it only when he needed a backup gun, sticking to his "unofficial gun" most other times.

The other gun was much the same, but this one was a stainless-steel K-Frame Model 65. It was already loaded as he took it from the Safariland shoulder rig—.357 Magnum 158-grain semijacketed softpoints. He opened the cylinder and gave it a good-luck spin, then stuck it back in the upside-down rig under the elastic.

He settled the holster onto his shoulders, then found his blue Windbreaker. He was glad for the lining. Riding the train through Colorado was cold work.

He jabbed his wallet, badge and ID case, keys and a fresh handkerchief into his trouser pockets. Then he checked the jacket to see that the Safariland speed-loaders were secure. He carried six rounds in .38, as well, but only because he was supposed to. He slipped on the Windbreaker and started for the front door of the caboose.

A biting wind hit him in the face as he opened the door. "Damn," he muttered through his teeth, closing the door and stepping across the little balcony to the next car forward. He entered the baggage car and closed the door behind him. It was time to inspect the troops.

THERE WAS TOO MUCH government waste, he thought, standing beside Ed Bartolinski in the forwardmost of the three freight cars. They stood on the little balcony; the spare engine's headlight was just above and ahead of him.

"Those crates that are supposed to have the warheads in 'em," he said to Bartolinski. "Why the hell didn't the government load 'em up with something free, like rocks, instead of something expensive, like pipe?"

"I dunno," Bartolinski answered.

"I know you don't know, Ed. I don't know, either. I was just saying—"

"Oh," Bartolinski said, nodding. Jefferson turned and looked at him.

Jefferson's radio crackled, and he answered it, "This is a AB 34. Go ahead."

"Antinuclear demonstrators ahead of us. Local police just contacted us on the big radio. I can see 'em blocking the track."

"Yeah, I can feel the train slowing down, but have the engineer keep well back from the cops and the demonstrators. We don't want any trouble."

"Roger on that, Miles."

The transmission went dead, and Jefferson glared at the radio. "Roger, wilco, over and out and up yours," he snarled, putting the radio back in his pocket.

"You're in a great mood today," Ed Bartolinski told him.

Jefferson started to say something, then laughed, leaning out along the side of the train. Without binoculars he could already see the flashing Mars lights and the milling crowd. "Just ruins my disposition, that's all, Ed," he said, not looking back at his friend, trying to let the cold wind wake him up. "Demonstrators three times yesterday." He looked at his wristwatch. "These guys are early. It's only seven forty-five. Proves the adage, though—"

"What adage?" came Bartolinski's voice behind him.

Jefferson took his eyes off the tracks ahead and looked up at the snow-peaked mountains they were passing. "Early demonstrator gets the picket sign."

"That's the adage? That's a terrible joke."

"Yeah," Jefferson said, then fell silent. He would be glad when he dumped his phony cargo and the real one hundred nuclear warheads reached their destination. He looked to the other side of the balcony, at the mountain range that seemed to stretch as far south as the eye could see.

Somewhere beyond the range the missiles would wind up—safe, he hoped. That was the only rationale for all the aggravation of the decoy train and the damned crates full of pipe. The wind stung his face where he'd plucked the hair.

THE TRAIN HAD STOPPED. Jefferson now sat on the steps of the forwardmost baggage car. David Palms and Ed Bartolinski were standing beside him. The protestors hadn't left peacefully. There had been arrests. Then more protestors had shown up. They were coming by the carful as he watched from what he gauged as a quarter mile down the track. They had got no closer.

He felt Palms tap him on the shoulder. "Relax, Miles, this is just what we want. Plenty of publicity, plenty of delay, more time for those real warheads to get to where they're going and get repaired or whatever and put back on line.''

"Yeah, if the Russians ever found out we took a hundred warheads off the lineup, hell, they might launch an attack,'' Bartolinski added.

"Yeah. Or if terrorists found out the warheads were traveling by truck and only had some lousy air police and the driver crews guarding them.... Hell, what'd happen then?''

"Like I said before—''

"Early protestors get the picket signs?'' Bartolinksi asked.

Jefferson just looked at him. "No,'' he said, scowling. "Government waste. Like those pipes in the crates, instead of rocks. Why the hell did the government pay some jerk-off to make warhead detonators that start detonating during an electrical storm? Dumb.'' He almost spat the word.

Some people had asked him to leave the FBI and run for Congress in his home district of Pennsylvania. Considering some of the dumb things the government did when it came to wasting money, maybe he would. "Couldn't do any worse,'' he said aloud.

"What?'' Palms asked him.

He looked at Palms and grinned, then frowned at the demonstrators. "Thinking out loud is all, friend. Just thinking out loud.''

9

Track left the mountain highway behind him and turned the white 4x4 Ford Bronco onto the gravel-and-dirt road that led to his ranch house. He drove with the side window open, and a cool breeze rushed through the Bronco. The setting sun was visible as the ranch road rose and the terrain to his left dipped slightly. Track squinted at it, smiling.

Pine trees lined both sides of the one-and-a-half-car-width road as it followed an S-curve. Track made a sharp right, his rear wheels skidding a little. The Bronco fishtailed slightly, as it should. Then Track recovered the wheel.

He could see the low sprawling ranch house perched on the mountainside. The security gates were closed, as they should be. Track picked up the encoded radio-signal device beside him and pushed the buttons in a combination series without even looking. The gates opened; the Bronco never slowed, and as he passed through the gates, he pushed another button, and the gates closed behind him. He made another sharp right, turning the Bronco onto the concrete apron in front of the garage.

His fingers beeped another combination, and the garage door rose. He drove the Bronco inside slowly and shut off his engine, then worked the signal device again. The garage door closed behind him with a pneumatic hiss and a loud click. He thought the click was getting a little too loud and decided to adjust the cable tension. He spent fifteen minutes with the garage-door mechanism before he was satisfied.

He wiped his greasy hands on a rag. Then he took the keys from the ignition and grabbed his attaché case from the front seat. The case held his pistols, and Track now ripped the red Firearms tag from it. He crumpled the tag, murmuring, "Stupid," and dropped it in the wastebasket beside the tool bench.

He opened the Bronco's rear deck to get his luggage, glancing at his Rolex. Tassles would have been by to feed Dorothy and to drop off her typing from his new book. He opened the side door into the house, a stuff sack hanging from its strap on his left shoulder. He held the locked attaché case containing his pistols in his right hand.

He saw Dorothy from across the living room. She was sitting on the dining-room table. "Hi, Dorothy," he called out.

The cat meowed once.

He shrugged. It was more than he'd expected. He'd been gone only two weeks.

He set down the stuff bag and his attaché case and walked to his right, toward the double sliding doors leading to the fenced patio and the pool.

He heard something and turned around. Probably Dorothy, he thought, but Dorothy hadn't moved.

"Mr. Track?"

"Oh, jeez," he rasped, turning to his left. He saw a man with an Austrian Steyr submachine gun.

"Mr. Daniel Track?"

It was a second man, this one to Track's right, also carrying a Steyr.

"Mr. Dan Track who's just returned from London?" A third man came out of the kitchen, a silenced Walther P-38 in his left hand. He held the gun too casually, as if he were right-handed and the banana he was eating from his right hand was, for the moment, more important than the gun.

"I see Tassles made it by with my typing and fresh fruit."

The man with the banana and the Walther P-38 smiled. "I guess so. I saw the typing on a desk in the room facing the pool."

"Yeah, that's the place." Track nodded.

"And the bananas sure do taste fresh."

"Good," Track said, smiling. "Wouldn't want to blow my image as a perfect host."

"You know," the man with the P-38 said, "most people we come around to knock off aren't nearly so friendly. So gosh, I don't know."

Track smiled again. "Well, people have come around trying to knock me off before. So, you know, experience counts."

"How true." The man with the silenced Walther agreed. "Would you like to know who paid us to kill you? What about it? We're in no big hurry."

"Sure." Track shrugged and walked slightly forward. He heard the rattle of a sling swivel against metal as the two men flanking him moved their submachine guns to follow him.

The man with the banana and the 9mm moved down into the dining room, close to where Dorothy lay.

"Some guy sounded like somebody doing a Barry Fitzgerald impression."

"IRA," Track suggested.

"Guess so. He said you executed some guy named O'Malley. He wanted you to know that was why you were getting hit. Guess they didn't have any of their own people around to get you, so they hired us. We smuggle some explosives, stolen weapons, things like that. Smuggle them out of the country for the IRA. We told 'em it wasn't any imposition to ask us to kill you. Anyway, a couple thousand bucks in anybody's pocket is good these days."

"Amen to that," Track agreed.

"Times are tough," the man with the banana said. "Would you like it sitting down or standing? Your choice."

"How about running?" Track smiled.

"Hey, listen," the spokesman said, "it's good to deal with a pro—you know, keep your sense of humor in adversity. I like that. Laugh in the face of death."

"Yeah, that's me." Track grinned. "But I must warn you—make one move to harm me and she'll cut your eyeballs out, friend."

"Who, your secretary? She was gone before we even got here."

"No, she will." Track pointed to the half-snoozing Dorothy on the edge of the dining-room table.

The man with the P-38 turned to look at the cat for a brief instant. Track noticed one of the men with the Steyr also stole a glance at her. Dorothy opened her eyes and looked back at the men.

"The cat?"

"Yeah, you've heard of 'em." Track eased himself against the arm of an overstuffed reclining chair, a brown Stratolounger. He perched on the arm, the sub-gun muzzles following him. "I mean," he said, "well, everybody's heard of attack dogs. You know, with urban overcrowding, the economy—dogs eat a lot. Anyway, this outfit on the West Coast trains attack cats.''

The guy with the banana laughed. ''Her?''

Track sighed. ''Look, one pro to another. I'm trying to warn you. It was written up in *Time* magazine about a year ago. You miss the article?''

The man holding the Walther raised his eyebrows, taking another bite of the banana. ''What article?''

''You ever watch TV? A couple of those syndicated human-interest-type things had features about the place—Kelsoe's Killer Cats.''

''Bullshit,'' the man on his right snarled.

Track shrugged. ''You know how cats can jump. They go right for the face, the eyes. In that magazine article there was a police photo of a guy who tried to knock over a liquor store where one of Kelsoe's Killer Cats was on guard. Jeez, the face.''

Track swallowed hard, and his right hand drifted toward the wooden handle on the right side of the Stratolounger—the handle that extended the footrest. He started moving the chair under him, rotating it only slightly back and forth on its revolving pedestal. ''So don't go slapping me with a lawsuit afterward. You've been warned,'' Track concluded.

The man with the Walther had finished eating the banana. He set the peel down now next to Dorothy on the dining-room table—but not too near her—then said, ''Okay, Track, enough bullshit. You're getting it.''

''Sic 'em, Dorothy!'' Track shouted.

The man wheeled toward the motionless bored- looking feline. So did the man to Track's right. Track pressed back and down on the wooden handle of the

Stratolounger; the footrest sprang with a loud twang.
He launched himself at the man to his right, swiveling
the chair hard left as he moved. The footrest smacked
against the shins of the man to his left. Glancing back,
Track saw the man grimace in pain.

Track's right shoulder made contact against the man
on his right. The Steyr fired wildly into the low ceiling,
and plaster rained down as Track got his balance. He
snapped the heel of his right hand into the subgunner's
jaw, at the same time half wheeling right, his left foot
kicking up into the subgunner's right forearm, impacting the arm and subgun against the man's rib cage.
Track finished the rotation and balanced now on his left
foot. He back-kicked with his right into the subgunner's
face. The man fell backward, his head hitting a low
table with a sickening crunch.

The second subgunner was strafing the wall as Track
dropped into a crouch. He rotated half right and
wrenched the Steyr out of the unconscious man's hands.
A vase beside Track's head on the bookshelves shattered
as the man with the silenced Walther opened fire.

Track had the subgun now. He sprayed it across the
room to give himself a break from the gunfire coming at
him. He rolled to the right and came up on his knees,
the subgun clutched tight against his abdomen. He triggered a three-round burst that tore into the man with the
silenced Walther. The man went down.

The second subgunner was up, firing from behind the
sofa as Track hit the floor. Track squeezed the trigger,
but nothing happened. The Steyr had jammed.

He pushed himself to his feet then threw the subgun
toward the couch. His left hand reached out to the
bull's-eye center of a dart board that hung on the wall

behind him. He jerked a dart out of the board and switched it to his right hand.

The subgunner was standing; the SMG started to chatter into the wall beside Track as he threw the dart, snatched a second, threw it, then a third, throwing it, too. The man's weapon discharged into the floor and then into the ceiling as he screamed, "My eyes!"

Track took a running dive across the back of the couch, tackling the blinded subgunner. The man's eye sockets were leaking fluid as Track wrestled him to the floor with the Steyr between them. Track's right knee smashed up into the left side of the blinded gunman's head—once, twice, a third time. The screaming stopped; the body did not even twitch.

Track pushed himself to his feet and started walking toward the dining-room table. He bent down to pick up the Walther with the supersonic silencer attached. He checked that the slide lock was off, worked the hammer drop on the left side of the slide and, pointing the pistol toward a chair, let the hammer fall. On closer inspection he saw it was a P-43 with the newer safety system.

He worked the base of the butt magazine release, checking through the witness holes. There were six rounds remaining. He rammed the magazine back up the pistol's butt; the gun was ready for a double-action pull.

Then Track heard Dorothy meowing. Turning around, he saw her coming out of a bedroom. Track reached out and petted her.

He walked into the kitchen and dialed the police. He told them to send an ambulance. There'd be an inquest—he didn't need to waste the time.

He thumbed through the mail on his kitchen counter

as he set down the receiver. There were bills and a letter from his publisher. He opened it and found a confirmation letter, a copy of the completely executed contract and a check. He folded the check and put it into his wallet. There was a telegram. He opened it.

It was from Chesterton.

KLAUS GURNHEIM ESCAPED CUSTODY STOP BELIEVED TAKEN BY JOHANNES KRIEGER STOP TWO OFFICERS KILLED STOP BRITISH INSPECTOR MISSING STOP PLEASE RECONSIDER CARTEL'S OFFER STOP

He crumpled the telegram and left it on the counter.

He walked over to the fruit bowl and picked up a banana. Suddenly he realized he was hungry.

10

He studied himself in the lavatory mirror. The short blond wig and the gold earring in his left earlobe made his teeth seem vastly more prominent. He had hated piercing his ears, but it had been necessary.

Underneath the black leather vest he wore no shirt, only a half-dozen heavy gold chains. On his left forearm he'd body-painted a rose, which looked like a tattoo.

Another man entered the bathroom.

Krieger stepped back from the mirror, put his left combat-booted foot up on the toilet bowl and began to retie the boot lace. The skintight white jeans he had on hurt his crotch.

The guy who had walked into the bathroom was tall and chunky looking. He wore blue jeans, a black leather jacket, combat boots and plaid shirt. He began to comb his teased, shoulder-length brown hair.

"Hi," the man combing his hair said.

"Hi," Krieger said.

"Ain't seen you around."

"Don't get to 'Frisco much," Krieger said, smiling. He had finished with his boot and now stood beside the man, combing his own "hair."

"Good scene around here."

"Free, yeah," Krieger said, proud of his American accent.

"Can I buy you a drink?" the man asked.

"Sure," Krieger replied. They both finished combing their hair at the same time, and the man with the plaid shirt held the washroom door open for him. Krieger smiled, going through ahead of him. As they started toward the bar, he felt the man groping for his left hand. Krieger let him take it. His blue eyes were still probing the faces of the crowd—at the tables, at the bar, near the bandstand and the dancing couples, as well. All men. Yet he couldn't find the face of Jilly Mason.

With his new friend still holding his left hand, Krieger muscled in at the bar between him and a thin, overly made-up man. The man was talking animatedly with the bartender.

The big bartender, who was built like a bouncer and wore a see-through pink shirt, turned to Krieger and his friend.

"What would you like?" Krieger's friend asked him.

"Oh," Krieger said, laughing coyly, "whatever you're having."

"A Singapore Sling."

"Fine," Krieger enthused.

"Make it two, then, please."

The bartender nodded and walked away.

Krieger scanned the bar in greater detail. He finally saw Jilly Mason.

"Would you like to dance later?" Krieger's friend asked him.

Krieger played with the chains around his neck. "Sure, later," he said, nodding.

His friend was groping him. Krieger let him do it, feeling the man's hand on his buttocks; Krieger's mind was focused elsewhere.

Krieger knew Jilly Mason well. He was slightly built, short and had never been anything but openly gay. He was the best helicopter gunship pilot Krieger knew. Krieger watched Mason's thin, high-cheekboned features, his prominent forehead, the hair combed down to hide the recession of the blond hair from the face. The eyes were black. Two vastly larger men flanked Mason on either side; Mason's back was to the bar rail. They were arguing.

"Where you from?" It was Krieger's friend.

The drinks arrived, and Krieger answered, "Down in L.A.—but I like the scene here."

"You come up here alone? I mean, no old man?"

Krieger smiled. The man stopped groping him. "No, I got no old man," Krieger said.

The groping started again. The friend's left hand held the Singapore Sling. "Toast, to us?"

"Sure," Krieger said, clinking glasses with the man beside him. He sipped at his drink. It tasted like urine, he thought. He set the drink down, turning to the bandstand. The group was starting into a fifties routine. The lead singer had on a pink sweater and poodle skirt, but the girl singer wasn't a girl.

"Wanna dance now?" Krieger's friend asked.

"No, let me finish my drink. This is delicious."

"Okay, honey," the man said.

Krieger looked back down the bar at Jilly Mason and the two big guys who were bracing him. One of the men reached out, knotting his right fist into Jilly's hair. Jilly slapped him. The man holding Jilly's hair yanked on the hair, snapping the head back as the second man backhanded Jilly across the mouth.

"That go on here a lot?" Krieger asked his friend.

"What, fighting? Yes, you know how some guys are— cats."

"Yes," Krieger nodded. Mason seemed unable to protect himself. He was running true to form—always poor in a fight.

Krieger turned to look at his companion. "Darling, I just decided—you're not my type." His left hand reached out and pulled on the wide-belted waistband of his friend's jeans. With his right hand he poured the Singapore Sling inside the front of the man's pants.

"Bitch!"

Krieger brought up his right knee as he turned, ramming it into the man's crotch. As the man doubled over, screaming, Krieger worked the right knee again—into the man's face. With the side of his left hand he executed a swift chop across the back of the neck. The man sank to the barroom floor.

Krieger stepped away from the bar toward the two men who were hassling Jilly Mason. They turned around, and the nearer of the two came at him, a little uncertain. Krieger feinted an obvious punch with his left. The man started to block it as Krieger's right hand—still holding the glass—slapped forward, smashing the glass across the bridge of the man's nose. Krieger let go of the glass just in time to avoid cutting his fingers. White cartilage began to spot red. Then blood gushed freely from the large cut on the man's nose. Krieger wheeled half right, snapping his left foot up and out, slamming the combat-boot's sole against the first man's chest.

There was fighting and screaming everywhere now as he let the man fall. His right foot snapped out backward, mule-kicking the man in the side of the head, putting him out hard.

The other man who'd been harassing Jilly Mason wheeled. A switchblade appeared in his right hand. There was a loud click as the blade shot up from the handle and locked into place.

Krieger reached to the bar and grabbed an empty wine bottle. He slapped the base of the bottle against the edge of the bar. The base shattered, leaving him with a jagged weapon.

The man with the switchblade took a step backward, gauging his opponent, then started forward. Krieger tossed the bottle into his left hand, feigning a lunge. The man dodged the thrust. Krieger wheeled to the left, snapping his foot up into the man's face. The man reeled under the impact as Krieger finished the turn, his left, combat-booted foot striking out for the inside of the man's extended right forearm.

The switchblade spun out of the man's hand. Krieger, switching the broken bottle back to his right hand, took a long step forward on his left foot, leaning into his adversary. His left fist smashed straight into the center of the face, while his right hand, still gripping the bottle, rammed forward into the abdomen, just below the sternum. His opponent shrieked as Krieger pulled back his arm, ready for another thrust. His right arm snapped forward, plunging the jagged edge of the bottle into the exposed throat.

Krieger dropped the bottle and let the body fall back flat on the floor.

Jilly's dark eyes looked at him.

"Who the hell are you?" Mason hissed.

Krieger sensed someone running toward him. He turned, punching out with his right hand. The man tried to dodge but was not swift enough. The middle knuckles of Krieger's fingers impacted against the base of the nose, breaking it, driving it up through the ethmoid bone and into the brain. The man fell over dead.

"Who do you think I am?" Krieger asked in his German accent.

"Johannes?"

"Let's get the hell out of here," Krieger snapped.

He shoved Jilly Mason toward the front door. Krieger could hear a police siren now as he followed Mason up the low steps, bursting through the door.

They collided with a uniformed San Francisco cop, his gun drawn.

Krieger's kick caught the officer under the chin, snapping the head back; the neck broke with an audible crack.

Krieger picked up the gun and tossed it away, half dragging the limping Mason.

"I can't run in these cowboy boots. The damn heels are too high," Jilly Mason complained.

Krieger kept pulling him toward the rented car. It was still parked at the curb half a block away. Krieger was running, occasionally looking behind him, as Jilly Mason stumbled along beside him. A police car was coming up the street, its roof lights flashing. Krieger found the car keys in the left front pocket of the tight-fitting white jeans. He jammed the key into the door lock and opened it, shoving Mason across the front seat.

Krieger flipped onto the hood and executed a body roll across it, landing on the driver's side. Mason already had the door open for him.

Krieger threw himself behind the wheel. "Down," he shouted, ducking below the level of the backrest. The sound of the siren rose and fell in intensity as it passed.

Krieger sat up. He inserted the key into the ignition. "It's all right now, Jilly. Just relax and sit here beside me. If any cops see us, they'll think we're just out on a date or something."

"Krieger, but you look so—"

"Good to you?" Krieger smiled, glancing at Mason before he pulled out into the street.

"I never knew you were—"

"I'm not, of course. But the last time you saw me, I was dressed as a Catholic priest. I'm not religious, either."

There was little traffic. Krieger drove the stolen rental Ford close to the parking lane so a police car could pass him.

"There is a job, Jilly. It is of the greatest importance to the right—our right."

"The movement?" Mason asked, breathlessly.

"Yes, and it requires the most consummate helicopter pilot who exists, so I naturally came looking for you. The underground knew your haunts. There wasn't time to wait near your apartment, I'm afraid. Good thing for you I didn't . . . those two leather boys looked as though they didn't like you."

"Ah, a couple of—"

"Never mind, Jilly," he said, sighing. Sometimes the life-style of the men he worked with disturbed him. He reached up to scratch at his left earlobe where he'd pierced the ear the night before. It itched, but he didn't scratch it in case it bled.

"Johannes, whatever . . . to further the cause . . . I will do it."

Krieger nodded. He had known that.

11

George Beegh had driven through the night, letting Marvin Lundy sleep through a double shift. He was hoping to make himself tired enough so that he could rest no matter how much Marvin talked. There were two rigs in convoy so far; the other two trucks were due to join them just outside Albuquerque.

He smiled to himself as he read the sign, Welcome to New Mexico—Land of Enchantment.

"Land of secret arsenals where they repair nuclear warheads that don't work," he added, aloud. He wondered how that would go over on a welcome sign.

It was tedious driving that slowly, but hauling a half of a double wall meant slow driving because the thing was so wide. He felt it was the perfect way to transport the warheads. No one expected you to move fast.

The butt of the Colt Combat Government was biting into his rib cage again. He put his right hand between the gun and his shirt, rubbing at his flesh. Then he shifted the gun slightly.

He yawned, then glanced at his Rolex. He had bought the watch overseas when he'd served a year and a half of his six-year hitch with Air Force Intelligence. His uncle, the few times he'd seen him in recent years, had always worn a Rolex, and George had come to like the look of the watch.

He glanced at the watch again, having forgotten the time he'd read a moment earlier.

He frowned, returning his gaze to the road. The sun was up, but that didn't quite make sense with the time on his watch.

Then he remembered he'd had the watch set on Eastern Time, never bothering to change it in the Midwest, where he'd picked up the missiles. Now he was in the Pacific Time Zone—or was it Mountain? He shook his head. He couldn't remember.

He picked up his CB, punching down the talk button. "Pilot, this is Half-House."

He listened. "Cut the cracks, George."

"Hey, look, I'm pullin' over. It's Marvin's turn to drive, come back?"

"Gotcha. We'll find a spot on the shoulder just up ahead."

"Ten-four and out," he said, replacing the microphone on its rest. Smiling, he turned to look at Marvin. "You keep me awake this time I'll shoot you."

But Marvin just slept like a baby.

HE HADN'T SLEPT MUCH on the plane, and the police had kept him up until 2:00 A.M. They had gone over his story, dusted for fingerprints, even photographed the cat. He walked, trying to convince himself he should be awake. The shower hadn't helped and the six hours of sleep hadn't helped. He put it down to jet lag.

He was well away from the house, a little Chiefs Special stainless Model 60 tucked into his belt under his bomber jacket. The gun hung on a Barami Hip Grip. He yawned.

Track owned 17.32 acres of land. He remembered the exact number because the numerals 1732 were George

Washington's birthyear and the square root of three. His mind worked like that.

He sat down now on the stump of an oak tree that had been struck by lightning the previous year. He'd been forced to cut down the tree.

Track stared across the large lake to the other side. There was a government-owned plant there. He didn't quite know what went on, but he knew it was government owned. The security pattern made civilian ownership impossible, government ownership obvious, despite the fact no one wore a uniform and the guards carried Uzi submachine guns instead of M-16s.

He had dressed in night gear once and headed across the lake in a rubber raft. He had anchored the craft about three quarters of the way across, then swum in the rest of the way.

He had observed the guards there for more than an hour, then swum back out to his raft and rowed home. He had violated no laws. The lake was not private property, and the beach was state-owned land, as well. He had watched through binoculars from a tree that overlooked the compound.

He shrugged, taking a cigar from the inside breast pocket of his jacket. He clipped the end off with the little guillotine, then bit down on the cigar. He lit it and inhaled. Then he stood up and started to walk back toward the house.

He'd used the Aimpoint sight before, but only on handguns. He wanted to try some new mounts on an AR-15/M-16. And there were some other things he'd been meaning to test. The prospect of trying out new "toys," as he sometimes jokingly referred to them, was already getting his mind going.

Inside the house, he sat at the kitchen counter.

He secured the Aimpoint mount body to the carrying handle of the AR-15. The cargo pack on the floor beside him contained six loaded magazines for the AR. It would be more than ample for zeroing. Just a few shots, then some serious target practice.

"Serious target practice. . . ." He rolled the phrase on his tongue. He shot perfectly well. He always did.

From where he sat he could see the chalk outlines of the three dead men on the rug. There were bloodstains, dust and chunks of plaster from the ceiling. He had notified his insurance company, who'd promised to send out an adjuster in the next few days. He glanced at his watch. It would soon be time for his cleaning woman to arrive. She would be in and out again while he was out shooting.

Track stopped to pick up three boxes of new Federal Nyclad 125-grain semiwadcutter hollowpoint Chiefs Special load.

He would content himself with testing the ammo and the scope with the new mounts.

Track glanced at the Rolex again. There was time for one more cup of coffee, he thought. He walked across the kitchen and plugged in the electric kettle. As he waited for the water to boil, he began to feel better.

It would be good to do something.

"HEY, WAKE UP, GEORGE!"

George Beegh opened his eyes, looked at Marvin Lundy, blinked, then looked at him again. "Wha— what?" He'd been sleeping, he realized. He'd needed the sleep badly. He glanced at his watch. He'd been sleeping for less time than he'd wanted. "What is it, Marv?" he asked, his mouth feeling dry, hot.

"I figured I'd let you know. We're turning off from Albuquerque."

George sat up, rubbing his eyes. He found his peaked Jack Daniels cap and pulled it on against the sun. There were mountains to his right; to his left the land dropped sheer to the valley below. Wind socks were spaced at regular intervals along the highway. With each new gust they grew stiff for an instant, then flaccid, then stiff again. Now ahead of their pilot car were two trucks. On one he could read the name. He'd driven it once, or one like it. Like most men in the pool of nuclear couriers and guards, he had no idea how small or how vast his organization might be or how much rolling stock was available.

He looked in the mirror on his right, not seeing much but the half double wall they were hauling. He leaned to his left, craning his neck to get a view from Marvin's side mirror. The second double wall was there as it should be, as was the second pilot car. "Convoy's complete now," he muttered, his throat feeling dry and hoarse.

"Yeah. We turn off two miles ahead toward the arsenal. Then we rest easy for a while."

George Beegh nodded, settling himself back in his seat. "I can use that, all right." He shifted the butt of the Colt Combat Government again where it dug into his rib cage. "Yeah, I can use that," he said again.

There would be thirty-six hours to rest and unwind while one hundred warheads were repaired and had their detonation systems adjusted and tested.

He grunted, yawned, stretched, then closed his eyes.

12

The driver handed over the identification card.

The gate guard accepted it, studying it for a moment. Then he looked at the face of the man who had passed it to the driver.

The general watched the guard, a corporal in the Military Police. His only visible armament was a .45 Government Model in a Clarino military flap holster on his right hip.

The MP handed back the identity card, saluting. Then he asked, "May I be of assistance to the General, sir?"

He cleared his throat. "No, son, just making an inspection. I have to drop in unexpectedly once in a while. Just open the gates and let us pass through as quietly as possible—me and my inspection team."

"Yes, sir. But I am supposed to contact Colonel Arden, sir."

"Well, you go ahead and tell him Brigadier General Adam Fleyderman's here, then. If he wants, he can meet me down by the field, checking out your Air Cav readiness."

"Very good, sir." The corporal saluted.

He leaned forward over the backrest, a little closer to the driver. He nodded, giving a fast sharp salute. "I'll remember you in my report, Corporal."

"Thank you, sir!"

He nodded to his driver then, his voice whiskey tinged and deep, said, "Phil, drive us on over to the field now."

"Yes, General," the driver said.

He watched as the gate swung open; the flags on the right and left front fenders stiffened as the car moved ahead.

Krieger exhaled hard, saying to Jilly Mason, his driver, "The general's voice is a difficult one. He drinks too much. Or should I say, he drank too much."

Jilly Mason laughed.

Krieger, without turning too much, glanced behind him. Two Jeeps loaded with men and another staff car brought up the rear.

Krieger settled back, lighting one of General Adam Fleyderman's noxious-smelling cheap cigars. He inhaled hard to get the odor onto his breath, exhaling the smoke across the chest of his uniform blouse, then wrinkling his nose at it. As they drove the post streets, he noticed uniformed men and women stopping to salute. Krieger dutifully returned salutes lazily.

The airfield would be another secure area. He puffed on the cigar again to keep the smell going as the car turned right. He looked ahead; the airfield gates were closed. Two MPs with M-16s stood at the gate.

The staff car slowed, then stopped. Jilly hopped out, opening Krieger's door. Krieger stepped out, straightening his uniform tunic. The MPs stiffened, going to present arms.

Krieger, inhaling his cigar, looked across at the men and returned the salute. "You men stand easy...looking sharp. Phil," he said to Jilly Mason, "show these soldiers my orders." Krieger turned away, and from the corner of his eye, he saw Jilly Mason produce the orders.

Krieger surveyed the two Jeeps and the second staff car, looking beyond them across the base. Exhaling loudly, he said, "God, I love this Colorado weather. The air up here—" and he sucked loudly on his cigar "—is worth breathin'. Not like at the Command School in Kansas. Air there smells like cowshit all the time." He turned and walked past Jilly Mason and the two MPs. One of them was perusing the orders.

He stopped at the gates, hooking his fingers on the chain link and staring across the field. Without looking back, he addressed the senior of the two MPs by name—he'd read the name tag. "Sergeant Cummins, think this here Air Cav outfit can stand a quick inspection and come out looking as sharp as you and that private?" He didn't glance back.

"Yes, sir!"

Krieger turned around. He extended his hand for the orders. "Good, then open the gates. And give Colonel Arden a call for me. Tell him to clear his calendar for this afternoon. I'm buying him lunch."

"Yes, sir." The sergeant snapped to a rifle salute at sling arms. Krieger returned the salute and took the orders back, handing them to Jilly Mason. Krieger started for the open back door of the staff car. He stepped inside, settling back and puffing on his cigar. Mason closed the door.

The two MPs went to present arms again as Jilly bounced into the front seat and put the transmission in drive. The staff car started forward. Krieger nodded to the MPs as the gates swung open. The car picked up speed, heading across the field.

Ahead, Krieger could see the main hangar. "Drive that way, Jilly," he said in his own voice.

"Yes, Johannes, I mean, General." Mason laughed again.

The four vehicles drew up to the main hangar, and all the occupants stepped out. They entered the building.

Krieger strode across the central space of the main hangar, followed by his other officers, all carrying clipboards. Each man in the "inspection team" also carried an attaché case. Krieger inhaled, glancing up at the nearest of the Sikorsky CH54B Tarhes. His eyes took in the small, three-man cockpit, the girderlike fuselage and the massive six-blade main rotors.

Each selected pilot had flown the CH54B.

"Ascertain the readiness status of these aircraft, Colonel," Krieger said to the officer nearest him. His staff officer turned to the knot of ground-crew personnel standing at the far end of the hangar.

"You, there, Sergeant!"

"Sir!" The fatigue-clad sergeant started to run over.

Colonel Arden had joined them and was now standing on Krieger's left. He nodded approvingly. "Your men get things going mighty quick, Colonel."

"Thank you, General," the colonel said, smiling.

"Four CH54Bs and one AH-1Q TOW Cobra and three Huey 214Bs. You've mustered them out quick, Colonel."

Krieger's men were already aboard each of the eight machines, inspecting flight readiness. The beating of the rotors sounded like a swarm of giant insects.

Krieger turned to Arden, smiling, then walked toward the hood of his staff car. He could feel Arden near him.

"General, if I may ask, sir, why just these specific aircraft, sir? I mean, we could really show you—"

Krieger had his attaché case open; the silenced Walther P-5 was in his right fist as he turned around. He spoke in his own voice. "I'm a terrorist, Colonel, and these eight machines were all I required. Thank you very much."

The first round from the 9mm P-5 punched a neat hole between Colonel Arden's eyes just under the peak of his uniform cap. The cough of the silenced shot was inaudible over the beating of the rotor blades. The body fell backward.

Krieger closed his briefcase, holding the silenced pistol against his right thigh as he started walking toward the Cobra gunship.

Men were starting to move. Krieger heard a single shout. "It's the colonel—"

Another, "Maybe it's a heart attack."

After a moment there was a loud shout, louder than all the rest. "Jesus—Colonel Arden's been shot in the head!"

Krieger smiled, turning around, dipping his head under the rotor blades perfunctorily. Jilly Mason rolled the body of the pilot out onto the airfield tarmac.

An MP was fumbling for his .45 auto in its full-flap holster. Krieger raised the silenced P-5, aimed it leisurely as the MP worked the slide of the pistol to chamber a round so he could fire. Krieger fired first.

Red splattered over the white scarf at the throat of the MP's uniform. The left hand clutched at the Adam's apple, which Krieger had used as a target.

Krieger climbed aboard the Cobra as Jilly Mason began to work the stick. The rotor speed increased. Then the craft was airborne.

Krieger looked right and left. The CH54Bs were already lifting off, going low across the field away from the main hangar and the smaller hangars that made up the complex on the field. The 214Bs were also airborne now. Krieger reached across and snatched up the headset, pulling it on over his hat. "This is Johannes Krieger. Initiate plan Alpha, initiate Alpha." Then he glanced at Jilly Mason, tapping him on the shoulder.

Mason looked at Krieger as he signaled with his right thumb, jerking it upward. Mason nodded, smiling. His hat was gone, and his blond hair blew in his eyes from the healthy wind whipping into the cabin through the craft's open side door.

The helicopter spun and climbed as Jilly Mason expertly flicked the arming controls on the four round pods for the TOW missiles.

Mason looked to Krieger. Krieger nodded. There was a rumble from starboard as Mason triggered the first missile. The TOW missile fired, its contrail snaking after it. Suddenly the main hangar erupted in a fireball of orange and yellow; a cloud of heat and fire scorched upward. The 214Bs were in position. Antitank missiles discharged in clusters toward the smaller hangars and other aircraft still on the ground.

The hangars and helicopters were exploding. Men in full battle gear were running toward the helicopters. Pieces of bodies rained down as Krieger watched.

He spoke into his headset radio. "I want the ship piloted by Blackstone to break off, then level the post headquarters structure and knock out the radio and telephone communications. Then rendezvous as planned. Krieger out."

One of the 214Bs was streaking just above the ground

toward the center of the compound, an M-60 firing from its open portside door. Antitank missiles belching contrails rocketed at trucks moving out onto the field. The trucks seemed to vaporize.

Krieger tapped Jilly Mason on the shoulder again. He signaled thumbs up again. Mason laughed, and the helicopter lurched to starboard. Krieger spoke on the radio, "Attack elements break off. Pick up and fly cover on the Sikorskys. Krieger out."

He looked at the chewed stump of General Fleyderman's cigar. Somehow it reminded him of Mrs. Fleyderman's fingers after they had tortured her to get information out of her husband.

13

"Johannes," Jilly said, speaking to Krieger through the headset.

"Yes, Jilly?"

"They cannot help but hear us."

"What should cause them to suspect military helicopters until it is too late?"

"But what if the base— Oh, I forgot . . . the attack on the radio center and the headquarters."

"It should take at least another half hour before anything formidable can be thrown up against us. And by then. . . ." Krieger let the sentence hang.

"What if they get contacted—the convoy, I mean, Johannes?"

Krieger, unbuttoning the blouse of his brigadier-general uniform, shook his head. He stared through the canopy of the chopper at the small fleet around him. "The likelihood of such fast action is remote, exceedingly remote. And even if they expect us, what can they do? Turn around? Not those double-wall trailer halves they pull. Fight us? With what? Stop? For what? They can do nothing.

"One driver and one guard, alternating, in each vehicle. Eight all told. Two men in each of the two pilot cars for the double-wall trailer halves. Another four men. One dozen men—four of them air policemen who are doubtlessly heavily armed, eight of them nuclear guards who carry individual side arms. Against eight helicopters—four of which are heavily armed—rockets, missiles, miniguns.

"What can they do, indeed? Take a chance on detonating one of those extremely fragile warheads and blowing a huge crater into the middle of northern New Mexico? Blow them all up? Create an electromagnetic pulse that would destroy all communications, engine magnetos, electrical power? Wipe out much of the Southwest, kill millions? What can they do, Jilly?"

Jilly had no answer.

Krieger expected none.

14

Dark silhouettes above the horizon were drawing George Beegh's attention. His gaze kept alternating between the road and the sky. "Hey, Marvin? Marvin!"

George Beegh shot a glance to his right. Marvin was sound asleep. He took his right hand off the gearshift and slapped Marvin across the left arm. "Marvin. Dammit, Marvin!"

"What, huh?"

George looked at him again. He was starting to wake up. With Marvin, George reflected, you could never be sure of anything, especially consciousness. "Marvin, wake up, dammit!"

"What?"

"Marvin, what the hell do those look like?"

"What?"

"Those," George insisted, freeing his right hand of the gear lever again and thrusting his index finger skyward. "Those!"

"They look like Army helicopters, maybe. Don't see many of those big crane-fitted cargo choppers. Those are the big ones. I read once they can lift twenty tons or more. I don't know what the smaller ones are."

George counted the praying-mantislike silhouettes, looming larger now. There were exactly four of them, flanked by four smaller helicopters. There were, he rea-

soned, exactly four rigs hauling the nuclear warheads.
Those big choppers could—

"Holy cow," George whispered, his voice barely audible. There was a little vapor trail coming from one of the smaller craft. He picked up the CB mike. "Hey, look up there, guys, look—"

The pilot car immediately in front of him exploded. He could swear he'd seen a missile strike it.

The fireball from the pilot car belched upward, caught on the wind. It licked toward them.

George wrenched the wheel hard left, into the oncoming lane. The half double-wall trailer behind him fishtailed wildly as he recovered the wheel. He upshifted to pick up speed, downshifting when it did no good, double-clutching and downshifting again. The fireball was abreast of the truck's cab now, directly to his right. George double-clutched and upshifted; the engine throbbed maddeningly loud. The engine's roar was more like a loud purr now as the rig shot past the burning car.

George cut his wheel gently right, back into the right-hand lane. The blazing Mustang with the two air police inside was left behind. The smaller helicopters were closing fast. He wound the driver's-side window all the way down.

Above the whirring of the rotor blades a German-accented voice was speaking on a public-address system. "On the road, nuclear convoy, surrender now and you will be spared!"

George sneered skyward, reaching for the Colt on his right hip. His right hand found the Pachmayr grip of the pistol, and his fist wrapped around it.

"Hey, George!"

"Shut up, Marvin," George shouted over the roar of

the wind rushing past them. Thumbing down the safety, he aimed the pistol as best he could toward the helicopter above them. "Fuck you!" He fired twice, then flipped the safety, jabbing the pistol back in its holster. He focused his eyes once more on the road. The two semitrailer trucks were ahead of him, making better time because they were more maneuverable and could travel at higher speeds.

The helicopters were zigzagging at treetop level through the sky overhead; the occupants were visible from time to time. Machine-gun fire ripped into the road just ahead of them, as if trying to force them to stop. He saw U.S. Army uniforms. He didn't believe it was possible.

"Those are our guys up there!" Marvin shouted.

"Oh, yeah?" George sneered. "Then what the hell are they shooting at us for? And with what we're carrying!" He didn't wait for an answer but built his rpm on the tach, fighting the grade with more gas. In the side mirror he saw the contrail of another missile. An air policeman was leaning out of the window of the second pilot car, firing an M-16 skyward. Then the man, the M-16 and the car were replaced by a fireball. George scanned his left-side mirror and saw the second of the two half double walls skirting the burning wreckage. The rig was in the left lane, coming up fast.

The voice came from the air again. "This is your last warning. You must surrender now and no one will be harmed!"

"Lousy son of a bitch!" George shouted. He reached to the CB, flipping the PA switch. Picking up the microphone, he hit the talk button. "You lousy son of a bitch!" he shouted into the mike. His voice echoed and reechoed across the road as he drove, ricocheting off the mountainside.

The smallest of the four attacking helicopters was coming in for a close pass. The German-accented voice on the PA system said, "You, I will kill!"

George stomped down harder on the accelerator. He caught a glimpse of a yellow road sign showing an S-curve dead ahead. "Aw, great! Just what I don't need."

He started downshifting. The S-curve sign had been posted 35 mph. There was a roar of engine noise to his left, and he snapped his head to see what it was. The second of the two half double walls, the cab scorched and the guard hanging out of the side window, was coming fast.

"Hey, what happened to Maurice?" Marvin shouted.

"He's dead, you idiot," George shouted back. The truck cab was weaving from right to left. The cab's right fender crunched into the double wall George was driving.

"What?" It was Marvin again. "Must be something wrong with Ted, too!"

The truck was coming faster now into the curve, and the cab was almost dead even with George as he looked out. He could see Ted, the driver, with one hand on the steering wheel, the other hand over his eyes.

"Marvin, slide over when I jump out. I'm going to help Ted," George shouted. He reached up and pulled down the peak of his Jack Daniels cap. Then he fastened the hammer strap on his holster so he wouldn't lose his .45. He moved his right hand to the stick, double-clutching and downshifting. The two cabs were even now as he glanced left. "Take her, Marvin!"

George worked the door handle, stepping out onto the

elevated running-board steps. His right hand still gripped the wheel. Then he felt Marvin take it. He let go, glancing down. If he missed, the wheels of one of the trucks would get him.

He reached out his left arm. His right hand was anchored to the doorframe. His left hand groped for the right side mirror of the other truck. He was not close enough. "Marvin," he shouted. "Get me closer, then pull away and slow her down when I jump!"

"Get yourself killed, George!"

"No kidding!" George shouted back, extending his left arm as far as it would go. He felt his balance shift as Marvin steered closer to the second cab. "Now or never," he coached himself. Letting go of the driver's-side door, he jumped.

He hadn't jumped far enough, he realized, as his left hand slipped. His right hand groped for the frame of the mirror as he felt himself being pulled away in the slipstream. Then his right fist closed on it, and the frame of the mirror sagged under his one hundred eighty pounds. His left hand reached out—for anything except the vertical exhaust pipe that traveled up the side of the cab behind the doorframe. It would be too hot to touch, let alone hold.

He threw his body left and in toward the fuel tank. His cowboy-booted feet dragged for an instant. A spare wheel was wired down just forward of the fifth-wheel connection. He groped for the spare wheel with his left hand. He let go of the broken mirror framework as his left found the rim of the wheel.

Struggling, he pulled himself across the fuel tank toward the driver's side. Heat from the engine blasted him as he fought to gain his footing. Then his feet found the framework leading to the fifth wheel, and his hands were on the cab roof.

He could see Ted now with the steering wheel still held in one hand. Ted was screaming, rubbing his eyes.

The windshield in front of the driver was shattered, blown inward.

Sweat poured off George as he reached his hand up across the cab roof to the twin air horns. He grabbed at them, tugging firmly. They held. He moved his right hand down from the air horn to the door handle. "Ted, slide over, I'm coming in!" George shouted. Ted still screamed.

George wrenched at the door handle. The door sprung open, and he swung out with it as he lost his footing. His body was suspended over the road. He looked down. Suddenly there was no road, just a sheer drop down the valley. His left arm was hooked through the window opening, while his right hand swatted at the top of the doorframe, trying to get a grip. Then he had it. With his left leg he kicked out at the body of the cab, trying to close the driver's door partially.

More gunfire came from overhead, strafing the highway around him. He glared upward, then kicked again. The door started to swing shut with the force of the slip-stream.

His right hand grabbed the assist handle beside the doorframe, and he wrenched the door handle once more. The door flew back as he kicked it open. Ted had both hands over his eyes as he fell out the door screaming, "I wanna die!"

George hung there for an instant, shouting, "No, Ted, no!" But Ted had disappeared over the cliff.

The rig was zigzagging badly now as George threw himself inside. His left hand snaked out to find the wheel even before he was seated upright. He straightened himself, finding the pedals with his feet. Staring ahead, his jaw dropped—he was into the S-curve.

George glanced at his right side mirror. It was darkened and soot stained, but he could see Marvin's rig slowing. Then it was gone from view as George cut the wheel into the first turn. He started downshifting, building engine compression to slow himself, working the brakes. The air brakes hissed madly.

One of the helicopters, its machine gun firing from the open door on the left, was dipping toward him. He cut the wheel farther right, getting into the center of the highway; his speedometer still hovered near fifty. The half double wall behind him whipped from side to side, crashing and dragging against the rocks on the right.

The gunship fired a burst across the hood. George ducked, wrenching the wheel involuntarily. But the rocks were coming up too fast. He tugged at the steering wheel—it wasn't responding fast enough. He stomped his right foot on the brake pedal and threw himself down to the floor as he tried to remember a prayer.

TRACK TESTED the new Federal Nyclads for the Chiefs Special. They printed tight at ranges to twenty-five yards—the peak of his marksmanship with a two-inch barrel—and functioning was as he had expected. He was opening the second box of hollowpoints when he heard what sounded like a missile detonating.

He loaded the revolver then stuffed it in his trouser band, grabbing the AR-15. He jammed a 30-round magazine up the well, snatched the cargo bag in his left hand and started to run.

Track stopped. The tree cover thinned as he looked overhead. He confirmed the sounds he heard when he entered the woods. They were U.S. Army-marked helicopters. He heard more missile firings and then machine-gun fire. M-60, he guessed, likely a doorgun. He counted four gunships, three the same. The fourth of the ships he pegged as a Bell. He watched the TOW missile firing. Then he knew for sure. It was a Cobra.

There was a gunfight on the road below him—but why?

Track worked the bolt on the AR-15, moving the selector to fire. He started to run again through the sparse woods. Tree branches swatted at him. He brought the rifle up, using it to bull his way through.

He broke tree cover, running faster now across a meadow toward a rock promontory from which he could see the road. He started up into the rocks, dropping as one of the 214-series helicopters swept overhead.

He looked up at the growing outlines of huge insect-like shapes in the sky. They were cargo choppers, but he couldn't remember the designation.

Rolling onto his belly, he edged up the rest of the distance along the rocks to the lip and peered over. Beneath him was a wreck. A half double wall was flipped onto its side against the rocks; the cab was smashed. Men in fatigues—evidently from a helicopter landed in the middle of the road—were extricating the occupants of the cab.

Track peered down, moving closer to the edge. One man was dead, his face blackened with burns. He saw a second man—tall, lean looking. He wore a cowboy vest and boots and a peaked Jack Daniels cap.

"Naw," Track told himself. "Couldn't—"

The cap fell off, and he saw the face. It was his late sister's son, George.

15

Johannes Krieger, lazily holding a silenced Walther P-5 in his right hand, stepped closer to Jilly Mason. "That is the one," he said to the pilot, gesturing with the Walther toward the man being dragged by two other men. "I can feel it. The one who called me—"

"That name," Jilly ended it for him.

"Yes, that name," Krieger said, laughing.

Then Krieger looked at the others. A blond-haired man who had been riding alone in one of the trailers appeared frightened. Krieger had made the men toss their guns in a pile on the ground.

"Throw him over there," Krieger ordered the two men carrying the third. They dragged the man toward the other prisoners, then heaved him forward. He fell to his knees, blood trickling from a wound on the right temple.

Krieger walked toward the pile of weapons, then stopped. He watched as the first of the Sikorsky sky cranes, with a McDonald's-marked semitrailer secured, lifted off.

One of the two men who had dragged the third presented Krieger with an automatic pistol.

Krieger glanced at it—a Colt .45. Then he looked up as a second Sikorsky moved off with one of the twin double-wall halves in tow on its crane.

He weighed the Colt in his left hand, then crouched, setting the pistol down. He examined some of the other guns, finally selecting one from the pile. "A .44 Magnum. Whose is this?" Krieger asked, rising to his feet. He stuffed the silenced P-5 into his trouser band under the webbed belt, shifting the nickel-plated .44 into his right hand. "I asked, whose is this?"

The blond-haired man who'd driven alone stepped forward, smiling. "Er, that's mine, sir."

"Hmm," Krieger smiled. He aimed the revolver at a tree trunk. "Does it kick much?"

"Like a mule if you're not used to it," the man volunteered.

"Interesting," Krieger said, appreciating the advice. Then he swung the muzzle toward the man, double-actioning the revolver. The big Magnum bucked hard in his right hand. The blond-haired man's face exploded, and his body sprawled back against some rocks.

"He was right, you know," Krieger said to Jilly Mason. Mason laughed.

"You son of a bitch!" screamed a voice from behind Krieger. Krieger turned back to the group of men. The one who had been dragged in was struggling on his knees. Two of his trucker friends were trying to hold him back. The black-haired young man shifted his body weight, and one of the truckers flew forward, sprawling. The kneeling man shifted his weight again, flipping the second man. He was on his feet now, charging forward. Krieger heard the clicking of safeties on M-16s held by his men.

Krieger raised the .44, cocking it. He pointed it at the approaching man. "Yes?"

The man stopped his charge, standing halfway between the knot of drivers and Krieger, nearly even with the pile of handguns.

"You are the one I want," Krieger said, smiling. "What is your name, young man?"

The man said nothing.

Krieger shifted the muzzle to one of the truckers. "I will shoot this man unless you answer me."

"George, George Beegh. B-E-E-G-H."

"George Beegh. What a name." He smiled at Jilly. Jilly laughed. Krieger looked back to George Beegh. "And, George, what do you plan to do, jump me and throttle me to death or steal a gun and start shooting?"

The younger man cleared his throat. "You're going to...kill—"

"All of you?" Krieger asked. "Yes, how perceptive of you. But you can make it more sporting. Jump for a gun, why don't you? Who knows, you might make it in time, hmm?"

The last of the Sikorsky sky cranes was airborne now. It was time to start the executions, to stop playing games, Krieger thought. "I'm weary of this." He raised the muzzle of the Magnum. "I must detonate my first warhead in the most poetic place."

Instead of jumping for a gun, the man named George dived left, grabbing for one of Krieger's fatigue-clad men. He caught the man off guard, hurling him toward Krieger. Krieger dodged left, his finger squeezing the trigger of the .44 Magnum. The gun bucked hard in his right hand. Krieger lost his balance, stumbling as the body of his man slammed into him.

He threw down the Magnum, grabbing instead for the silenced P-5 in his belt. He looked up to see George

Beegh running. Krieger raised the pistol and aimed. It would be a perfect shot.

DAN TRACK SKIDDED on his heels down into a grassy spot behind the rocks. He brought up the AR-15 to his shoulder. The safety was already off.

He sighted through the Aimpoint, steadying the red dot on the hand holding the silenced pistol. Someone was blocking Track's view of the gunman's body. Going for the hand was the only clear shot.

He guessed the range as slightly more than one hundred yards. He aimed a little higher than the target.

Track thought that if he missed— The pistol was aimed at his nephew, George.

Track fired.

The hand holding the pistol snapped up as the pistol flew through the air, discharging harmlessly. Track ducked as automatic-weapons fire hammered into the rocks above him.

Stone chips flew at him, one cut his right hand, which protected his face.

He rolled to the left and sat up, leaning his back against a huge boulder. He brought up the AR-15, waiting for a break in the gunfire. Then he stood up and peered over the rock ledge.

Below him he could see a group of men lined up beside the rocks. They were being executed. Track pumped the AR-15's trigger, sending two semiautomatic bursts into the men who were killing the unarmed truckers. He shot one gunman dead, wounding at least two more. Assault-rifle fire peppered the rocks near him. He ducked again as a movement on his left caught his attention. It was George. "George! Hey, George!"

The man turned, a look of fear mixed with determination on his face. "Uncle Dan?"

"Get down...in those trees...run for it!"

"No, the other guys down there—"

"They're dead already. Run for it, or we will be, too." Then Track was up and traveling. He snapped out a burst of long ragged shots, emptying the AR-15. He could hear assault-rifle fire behind him as he ran, but it was useless against him at the angle.

The helicopters' rotor beat was increasing. He knew the gunships would pursue him. Ramming a fresh magazine into the AR-15, then working the bolt, he kept running. He could see George ahead of him in the trees. The younger man turned around, waiting for him now. "Run, dammit, George. You never could follow directions, even when you were a kid."

"Shove it, Dan!" George called back.

Track laughed, moving into the tree line now. The rotor sounds were becoming louder still.

"Aw, jeez!"

It was George, looking skyward. Track didn't bother to waste time looking back; he knew what George saw. The gunships were airborne and coming after them.

Track just kept running, with George beside him now. The two men swatted their way through the trees, dodging low-hanging branches. Track's legs ached and his chest burned as his lungs screamed for oxygen. His mouth was wide open as he sucked air. His right hand clutched the AR-15; the cargo bag with the ammo was in his left.

Suddenly Track heard a whooshing sound above the throbbing of the rotor blades. He recognized the sound. "George, missile! Take a right angle to your left, fast!"

he shouted. Track angled to his right and ran faster now.

The impact threw him forward. His flesh stung as tree branches and rocks pelted at him. The rifle had skittered a short distance away from him. He tried to cover his head with his hands, burrowing his face in the dirt as gravel rained down on him. Then he felt a scorching heat, and he was up and running again.

Looking behind him, he saw the trees on fire. Then machine-gun bullets chewed into the ground around him. Branches were sawn away and came crashing down toward him. Track zigzagged through the trees, running for his life.

He glanced up behind him. One of the 214-series choppers was skimming the treetops, sweeping toward him. A gunner was leaning out of the door, firing an M-60. Track turned around, throwing himself to his knees. He brought the AR-15 to his shoulder, sighting the red dot on the man. Track fired three times. The man flopped forward, strung out across the M-60 as the chopper buzzed overhead and was gone.

Track pushed himself up, snatching a fully loaded magazine out of the cargo pack. He dumped the partially spent magazine, ramming the fresh one home. Grabbing the handle of the cargo bag, he began to run again.

"Dan!"

Track looked to his left and saw George breaking through the tree cover. Track shouted, "Keep running, but stick to the trees. Don't get in the open, George!"

Track heard the beat of the rotor blades again and looked up. It was the Cobra.

Track grimaced. He knew it would mean a missile.

The ground to his left dropped off suddenly. Track angled himself toward it, still running. There was a wide, swiftly flowing river below the sheer drop. He glanced back as he ran.

The sinister-looking Cobra was coming at him slowly, almost leisurely.

He could see the edge of the drop. He looked behind him again. This time he saw a contrail.

He launched his body forward into space, letting go of the AR-15 and the cargo bag. His arms and legs flailed wildly as the water rushed up to meet him. He was in midair when the impact from the missile came. He could see and feel the fireball as his body spun awkwardly.

Then he hit the water. He broke the surface, gasping for air. His eyes closed involuntarily, then opened again. His lungs ached from the exertion. His body was sore; his muscles burned. He dived again as a rain of gravel pelted at him.

Confused, he swam aimlessly, hearing popping noises as the gunship strafed the water about him. He kept down, and his lungs started to ache again. Then his feet touched bottom as the riverbank rose in front of him.

Track dragged himself up the side, his body suddenly cold and shivering.

He fell forward onto the sand, rolling onto his back. He brought out the Chiefs Special, raising it in his right hand. He squinted skyward against the brightness.

The gunships were breaking off. Track reasoned that they had something to guard, but he didn't know what.

"Uncle Dan!"

Track shook his head to clear it, then glanced behind him across the river. George was sliding down the embankment, coming after him. He lifted his arm weakly, then glanced up again.

He could see the helicopters traveling along the length

of the river, then rising. The Sikorsky sky-crane choppers looked like huge black insects against the blue cloudlessness of the New Mexico sky.

TRACK'S LEATHER JACKET hung on the back of a chair, drying. He had recovered the AR-15. It was dusty from the explosion but otherwise undamaged. The Aimpoint sight functioned perfectly. The Model 60, soaked in the river when Track had taken the dive, was already back in working shape. Track had removed the side plate immediately, using a hair dryer to remove excess moisture from the lock work. Then he had lubed the revolver. The contents of the GI cargo pack had been intact; the bag itself was covered with dust and light debris.

Track sat on the patio now, a Detonics Scoremaster .45 auto and his L-Frame Smith & Wesson on the table beside him. Next to these was a bottle of beer.

He had contacted the state police and the FBI immediately upon reaching the house. In both cases he did so anonymously, hanging up quickly.

He sat now, trying to piece things together.

George, wearing a pair of Track's jeans that were too short for him, walked out onto the patio to stand beside the swimming pool.

"You said one hundred—and they were five-hundred kiloton warheads with defective detonators?"

"Yep, that's what I said, Uncle Dan." George lit a cigarette and walked toward the table where Track sat.

Track raised his palm. "Let's back up a bit. When did you start driving these nuclear rigs?"

"More or less a year ago," George replied, sitting down across the table from his uncle.

"You realize you're stiffed any way you cut it."

"I know. If the Army, the Air Force and the NRC people believe me—that I am the only survivor because my uncle just happened to come along—"

"They'll throw you in the slammer, anyway, to keep your mouth shut and keep you safe," Track said, finishing George's sentence.

"Otherwise those terrorists will come after me. Maybe they unwittingly gave somebody a clue about what they're planning to do."

"Oh, I know what they're planning to do." Track laughed. "Blow the damn things up or charge a ransom—maybe both."

He looked at George. George looked at him. "This is great, just great. I'm twenty-five years old and I'm wanted by the government, by the terrorists."

"Good to be popular, son," Track told him.

"Popular, my ass."

"Yeah, well, remember when you turned twenty-one? Remember I told you someday maybe—"

"What? That we could work together?" George laughed. "You were talking about getting out of the Army."

"Yes, well, here I am," Track told him. "You still as strong as you used to be?"

"Why? You want the pool moved?" George joked, nodding toward the water.

Track laughed. "No, just thinking out loud. Only a matter of time until the FBI comes popping in and puts two and two together. They'll figure it was me out there. Then find you."

"What are you talking about, Dan? You don't mean—"

"Yes," Track nodded, chewing on his lip for a second, thinking. "Why not? Got something else to do?"

"You and me? Go after these guys ourselves? Sure I'd love to get those bastards for killing my friends. But how? I mean, we don't even know where to start. I know you make good money these days, but it would cost a small fortune just to try tracking them down. And we'd still have the law—"

Track stood up. "Wait a second," he said, walking over to the sliding glass doors leading into the house. He picked up a telephone and brought it back to the table, setting it down.

"We would need equipment, money and somebody to get the heat off us—" George was saying.

"Relax," Track told him. "You want to do it? I mean, really do it?"

"Yes," George said suddenly as he stood up, walking toward the pool. He dug his hands into his jeans pockets. "Lost my friends, lost my gun, even lost my damn cap! Yeah!"

"Good," Track said quietly. "Ever hear of something called 'The Consortium'?"

"The what?" George asked, staring at him.

"The Consortium—a big cartel of the world's largest insurance companies."

"No."

"Good, then you won't have any prejudices to overcome."

"What are you talking about? Insurance—what?"

Track didn't answer. He picked up the phone. He always wound up memorizing phone numbers, even when he didn't try. He hadn't tried with this one.

He dialed the eight hundred number to Sir Abner Chesterton's New York office.

16

Miles Jefferson hammered his fist against the side of the train car. "Dammit!" He looked at David Palms then at Ed Bartolinski. He looked at Bartolinski longer. "They what?"

Bartolinski smiled sheepishly. "Bunch of terrorists stole eight helicopters. Four of them were those big monster-sized cargo jobs. Everybody swears one of the men was Brigadier General Fleyderman. Anyway—"

Jefferson cut him off. His feet crunched the gravel near the tracks as he walked the length of the train car. The train had been stopped again. Quarter of a mile ahead the demonstrators were hooting and screaming. "They just waltzed right into a goddamn Army base and stole eight helicopters, then took a nice little flight a hundred miles or so—"

"One hundred eighteen miles," Palms told him.

"Right," Jefferson said, turning to look at the man. "Took this little one-hundred-eighteen-mile junket and just bodily picked up two double-wall trailer halves, a McDonald's truck and a—a—"

"United Parcel Service."

"Oh, yes, UPS, the Brown Army—right. So they picked up four...trucks, let's say." He turned around again, stopping his pacing, smiling. "We don't have to be that specific, do we?" Then he shrugged, his hands

raising at his sides palms upward. "So a gang of terrorists led by a U.S. Army general stole one hundred
warheads—each one about five-hundred kilotons effec-
tive yield. Let's see, now—"

"Two thousand megatons, Miles," Palms volunteered.

"Right," Jefferson said again, raising the index
finger of his right hand, jabbing it skyward, then staring
down at his size fourteen, wing-tip oxfords. "Right,
fifty megatons. That's enough to level, oh, say, New
York, Chicago, Los Angeles, Seattle, Atlanta, Den-
ver—whole bunch of places."

He laughed. Then he wheeled half left, his right fist
punching out into the side of the train. His knuckles
ached as he made contact, snapping his hand back.
"Damn!" He screamed the word. "If the Russians find
out we got one hundred missiles permanently off line,
who knows? Maybe they'll start an attack." His voice
rose and fell. "So what have we got? Seven dead
truckers, nuclear couriers, whatever. Eight dead air
policemen. One nuclear guard is missing. Some guy was
up in the rocks shooting an AR-15, we know that. And
we got one hundred warheads in the hands of a bunch of
terrorists led by a U.S. Army general."

"According to one of the survivors at the base, Miles,
well—"

"What?" he snarled, turning to Bartolinski.

"Well, the man swore the general took a pistol with a
silencer and shot the base commander in the head,
Colonel Arden." He closed his notebook with a loud
slapping sound.

"Oh, goody. We wouldn't want a rogue general who
does things halfheartedly, now would we? No, much

better this way. Every fucking terrorist—'' and he spoke slowly, spacing his words now ''—in the whole world is going to go after those warheads. Every third-world nation...instant nuclear preparedness. And they tell us, 'Go find them, guys. Don't alert the press, don't alert the local cops, don't even alert any other agents to the exact nature of what's going on.' Just us three pals go after one hundred warheads!'' He shook his head. His fist still hurt from the last time, but he hammered it into the side of the railroad car once more.

It hurt again.

17

Track had hidden George in the weapons vault when soldiers wearing radiation gear had come to the house. They said it was a reactor leak, nothing serious. But they had gone over the entire house with Geiger counters and other types of detection equipment. It had taken twenty minutes. During that time some of Track's guns had been seen, but a police officer who arrived with the soldiers recognized Track and calmed the tense situation.

As soon as they had left, Track raced to the weapons vault and opened it. George was headachy, almost reeling from the stagnant air in the vault. They had gone back to sit by the pool. George took deep breaths of fresh air.

No one else had come, but Track expected the FBI. If the local guys from the Albuquerque office appeared, it would be all right; he knew them.

He finally broke down and lit another cigar. George got up from the table and walked over to stand beside the pool, upwind of the cigar smoke.

It was 7:00 P.M. when Track looked at George, saying, "Hey, you still make great sandwiches?"

George nodded.

"Great. I didn't eat breakfast or lunch. I'll take three at least."

After a few minutes George returned with a tray of roast-beef sandwiches and beer.

Track ate three. Then he leaned back from the table. George was still on his second sandwich. "You don't eat like you used to," Track remarked.

George looked up, smiling. "Not as young as I used to be."

Track laughed. "Bull. I'm almost thirty-seven and you're twenty-five, so don't try to—"

"Hey—"

Track heard it, too, and grabbed the L-Frame .357. George had the Detonics Scoremaster out, and both men started toward the front door.

There was a car at the gates, then a horn beeping.

"Looks like a rental car," Track said, peering through the curtains.

"Yeah," George agreed.

The daylight was bad already and Track couldn't see inside, but then the dome light came on. "It is a rented car." Track smiled.

"So?"

"Guy driving it is Sir Abner Chesterton." Track went to the panel beside the front door to activate the gate-opening device.

18

Krieger had known that once the theft of the helicopters was connected to the theft of the warheads, the fuel range would be calculated in order to set up a preliminary search area. He had planned ahead for that, refueling the helicopters prior to the theft of the warheads, then proceeding.

After the warheads had been deposited at a chosen site, the aircraft were flown back into the search area. They landed at a point to make it appear as if lack of fuel made the landing necessary.

Trucks loaded with sandbags of the same weight as the missile warheads were waiting there. The trucks were driven to a desert area where the sand was carefully scattered. Once they reached a highway where their tracks could not be followed, the trucks returned to their point of origin.

Krieger, still disguised as General Fleyderman so none of his men would see his face and know his true appearance, stood now at the entrance to the sole hangar on the abandoned country airfield. He was immensely pleased with himself as he finished reviewing the beautiful simplicity and genius of his planning.

Jilly Mason was standing beside him, saying, "You have done it again, Johannes."

"Yes, I have," Krieger agreed. Then the corners of his mouth turned down. "Except for that young man who—"

"Called you that name," Jilly Mason put in.

"Yes," Krieger said. "The other one in the rocks who helped him escape—I'm certain the TOW missile killed him, and the machine-gun fire into the water would have finished the task if he had been only wounded. But the young man—I think he got away from us, Jilly."

Krieger started to walk down the center of the hangar. His men, more than a dozen of them, were already at work repacking the warheads. Each one of the warheads' defective detonators was removed under the personal supervision of Klaus Gurnheim.

Gurnheim looked up as Krieger passed him. Krieger waved, and Gurnheim called out, "If I wanted to work this hard, I could have got a steady job in a defense plant." Then Gurnheim laughed.

Krieger walked on. "Does he know anything, that young man who escaped. Did we say anything?" Jilly Mason asked.

"Nothing he could use. I made a vague reference to the site for the first detonation, but I doubt he understood me. He was more concerned about dying or escaping at the time, I'm sure. At any rate, it was such a slender clue. Even if it was properly understood, it would be—the American expression best serves—like looking for a pin in a haystack. And by the time the first detonation takes place, many of the other warheads will be out of the country."

"But how?"

"Relief supplies for underdeveloped African nations.

Medicine, typewriters, medical-analysis equipment and some other things," he added, deciding he had said enough.

"But surely customs will—"

"No, they won't. And several of the warheads will stay here, of course."

"But what do you plan to. . .what—"

"To restore the glory, to obliterate all enemies, to seize and hold supreme power, and these—" Krieger gestured expansively to the warheads "—these are the means, the keys to the kingdom, as it were."

"I don't understand," Jilly Mason began, lighting a cigarette. He reached out to touch Krieger's right forearm with his left hand, but Krieger moved his arm away, smiling.

"You are not supposed to—to understand it all."

"But you will detonate all of these?"

"No, unless, of course, that becomes necessary. Then I would without compunction. But, no, these early detonations are merely to make the world governments understand my sincerity."

"But—"

"Jilly, dear Jilly. The United States can tell no one these warheads have been stolen. Perhaps a handful of their agents will pursue me, but they do not even know it is me. They cannot trust the security of their allies. One leak and a possible attack from the Soviet Union. Certainly a war-alert status, DEFCON three or better—"

"DEFCON?"

"Defense Condition. DEFCON Five is war itself. But they can tell no one. What do the American fools tell their friends in Europe? Somebody stole one hundred warheads, fifty megatons' worth? 'We are sorry, but we promise not to let it happen again?' I doubt they can say anything. They cannot stop us, and soon they will realize that. And when I make my demands, they will agree. Or the planet will be useless cinders and rubble.''

"You really. . . would explode them all?''

Krieger stopped walking, turning to look at Jilly Mason. "Of course, Jilly, of course.''

19

"So what made you change your mind?" Sir Abner Chesterton asked, smiling broadly. He was sitting at the kitchen counter on the same side as Track, opposite to where George stood.

"Want a sandwich?" George asked.

"No, dear boy, but a drink would do nicely," Chesterton answered.

"What?"

"Whiskey and a splash. What you Americans would call Scotch and water. But light on the water, there's a good fellow," Chesterton told him.

Track watched Chesterton's face. "Sir Abner, let me ask you a question."

"Fire away, Dan. All ears, you know."

"Good," Track nodded. "What would be the liability problems if a five-hundred-kiloton nuclear warhead were detonated from a ground burst in a major U.S. city?"

"Good God, man, don't even think of such a thing."

"What would it be, the liability?"

"Why, billions of dollars. Let's say Manhattan, with Grand Central Station being ground zero, billions. Not to mention potential millions in lives lost. The liability incurred there would be staggering."

"How much did you want to pay me...to work for you?"

"One hundred twenty thousand per year, plus all expenses."

"Hmm." Track nodded. "How much would you pay him? He's my no-talent nephew George. Six years Air Force Intelligence, highest security rating they give. Almost one year as a nuclear courier for the NRC. Pretty good with a gun, but I'll make him better."

"Crap," George chimed in, laughing.

"And good in a fight, too. No martial-arts training, but a terrific street fighter. He's as strong as any two normal men."

"A package deal, as it were?"

"Right," Track said, sipping his beer.

"Sixty thousand and all expenses. I think I could get The Consortium to approve it."

"Only half of what he gets?" George asked.

Chesterton turned on his stool and smiled, saying to George, "There can be merit advances as time goes on, dear boy."

George nodded, smiling.

"I say, Dan, I noticed all the guns are out—or I certainly assume that's all."

"Most of them," Track agreed, glancing toward the living-room rug. The cleaning lady had got rid of the chalk lines the homicide people had left.

"A bit of trouble?"

"Last night. Some of O'Malley's friends paid me a visit. They died suddenly."

"Good show," said Chesterton, his eyes brightening.

"I'll need some special equipment. I'm class-three

licensed, but I don't own anything class three except an M-16.''

"We can certainly help there, Dan. Anything you need, short of an F-16 or a B-52." Chesterton laughed.

"Automatic weapons, other gear like that, I mean."

"No difficulty whatsoever."

"How much muscle would you have with the U.S. government, if you needed it? Really needed it?"

"Quite a bit, actually. If push came to shove as they say, I suppose The Consortium could always threaten to withdraw pool underwriting of the seventy or so thermonuclear power plants in the continental U.S., for a start.''

"Good," Track said. "What about NATO and SEATO nations?"

"We have considerable influence in those countries, as well. What's all this leading up to?" Chesterton asked. He took the drink from George, sipped it and smiled. "Your nephew would make a fine barman. Just the right touch of water."

"Thank you," George said.

"What's it all leading up to?" Track repeated.

"Yes, such a sudden about-face in your attitude toward coming to work for us. I mean, I'm overjoyed, but this rot about nuclear warheads and what-not—''

"Rot, hmm? Take a good healthy swallow of your drink first. Go ahead," said Track, smiling.

Chesterton finished half the glass, his face whitening, his left hand smoothing back his thinning gray hair.

"How about that sandwich?" George suggested. Track watched him, seeing that George was evidently enjoying it all.

"No, no sandwich," said Chesterton, his eyes locked

tight into pinpoints. He emptied the glass and handed it back to George. "But a refill of that, please."

"Once upon a time," Track began, "there were one hundred warheads, each five-hundred kilotons, with these cute little detonators that went crazy during electrical storms."

"Oh, my God," Chesterton whispered, his jaw dropping.

IT WAS NEARLY MIDNIGHT. Chesterton was unable to use the telephone, assuming all lines in the area would be tapped. When he'd told Track that, Track had agreed. They were sitting in the living room. Chesterton was on his fourth drink; he was dead sober.

There had been a long silence. Then Chesterton spoke. "I agree, Dan. The United States will not tell her allies—at least, nothing in detail. The news will be blacked out. The fact that George is still alive and you know the details—the FBI won't like that one bit."

"Can you pull their plug?"

Chesterton looked up. "I'm sorry?"

"Can you pull the plug on the Feds? Keep George free, keep them from getting after me? Can you get us a free hand?"

Chesterton seemed to think for a moment, then said, "I can—all of that. But don't expect any help. They'll resent your knowing, our interfering. They'll not aid us."

"Us," George repeated.

"Us," Chesterton emphasized. "I've come to another conclusion. With the two of you in the field, there'll be arrangements to be made, egos to smooth, feathers to unruffle. Coordination—that'll be my job.

And we could start doing our jobs if only we knew where to begin. Somehow we have to stop the terrorists from moving the warheads.''

Track glanced at his watch.

''By now, I'd say at least some of the warheads were on their way out of the country. We can't stop that. What interests me most is where the first detonation—''

''The first detonation?'' Chesterton interrupted, sitting forward in his chair.

George spoke. ''He said—''

''Who?''

''General Fleyderman or whoever the hell he was.''

''I think it was Krieger, Johannes Krieger,'' Track said.

''Who the hell is Johannes Krieger?'' George asked Chesterton.

''An international terrorist...right wing...Nazi. A man of the highest competency level, master of disguise. Not to sound trite, but he truly is. I'd say we'll find out shortly that General Fleyderman was murdered and Krieger substituted for him.'' Chesterton cleared his throat. ''But you were saying about General Fleyderman—or whoever,'' Chesterton said, looking at George.

''I was saying,'' George went on, ''that when he was holding Marvin's gun on me—''

''Marvin? Oh, yes, your companion guard,'' Chesterton interrupted.

''When he was holding Marvin's gun on me,'' George continued, staring off into space as Track watched him, ''he said something about a poetic place—the first detonation in the most poetic place.''

''Chicago,'' Track told him quietly.

"Chicago?" Chesterton murmured.

"Depending on what Krieger meant. If it was Krieger, and I believe it probably was, it could be Los Alamos or Bikini Atoll. Los Alamos would be too close to his operation to get the warheads in the first place. And anyway, not enough to destroy. Same goes with Bikini Atoll. It was blown up once, so why a second time? Only one other poetic place he could be talking about, unless he's figuring on Hiroshima or Nagasaki—and I don't think so. He'd want to hit America's jugular.

"It's almost impossible to take a train from any one place to another without passing through Chicago. And O'Hare is one of the busiest airports in the world. And Chicago's one of the three largest cities in the United States."

"The Manhattan Project," Chesterton whispered hoarsely.

"You mean, the first controlled nuclear reaction... during World War II?"

Track looked at George. Track nodded, licking his lips. "America started it all there."

"The Germans were working with the production of heavy water—"

"Deuterium," George murmured.

"Bright chap," Chesterton commented. "Einstein and some of the others petitioned then-president Roosevelt that the United States should undertake to construct a device that derived its power from the splitting of the atom."

"Stagg Field at the University of Chicago," Track said. "I used to hang around near there," he whispered, then looked at George. "When your mother was trying to raise her kid brother who was hanging around with the gangs.'' Track laughed.

"We could give that information to the FBI,'' Chesterton said halfheartedly.

"Let's,'' Track told him. "But not for thirty-six hours. That will give us twelve hours to get some sleep, then get to Chicago with the gear we need. Then twenty-four hours to get the ball rolling there. Who knows? Maybe if we need them down the line we can get their help.''

"Agreed,'' Chesterton murmured.

"George?'' Track asked him. "You want another Colt Combat Government?''

"Sure I do.''

Track looked at Chesterton. "Sir Abner, you just got started as coordinator. George needs a new pistol. I need some things. I'll type up a list of weapons and ammo for you later. Oh, and get George a class-three license right away. I mean real fast. We don't need federal weapons violations to slow us down.''

"All right, but—''

"We'll sack out here,'' Track interrupted, glancing at his watch. It was nearly 1:00 A.M. "You have four hours to rest, Sir Abner, then get on the phone. It'll be later in the East. Make your plug-pulling calls first. Then we can put through the other ones and not care who's listening. After that, start looking for the equipment. We'll also need a business jet standing by.''

"I flew here in one that belongs to The Consortium. I'll make arrangements.''

"Good,'' Track said, downing half his coffee, then setting the cup down.

He looked at George, then at Chesterton. "Later,

guys. Time for some shut-eye.'' He started across the living room, then turned. "Oh, one other thing, Sir Abner. Find me a guy in Chicago—his name's Rafe Minor.''

"An old friend who might help?'' Chesterton asked.

"Old friendly enemy who might help or might try to kill me—depends on his mood. He's the head of the Vandals Street Gang.''

"Vandals?'' Chesterton murmured.

"Vandals,'' Track repeated.

He picked up the L-Frame Smith from the kitchen counter, stuck it in the waistband of his trousers and started toward his room.

20

Vandals Enterprises, Inc. had its corporate headquarters located on Forty-seventh Street East. It was the headquarters for a string of car washes, fast-food chicken restaurants and a string of profitable numbers games and call-girl operations. At least Track had sufficient faith in his old friendly adversary, Rafe Minor, to assume them profitable.

As far as Track knew, Minor wasn't into drugs. He never had been when Track had grown up with him years before the Army.

The headquarters were on the second floor of a three-story building. On the third story was a dancing school and on the first a karate school, both run by Vandals Enterprises.

The black man driving the Cadillac was Walter Pembroke, a claims adjuster for one of The Consortium's member companies. Chesterton sat beside George in the back seat; Track was next to Walter Pembroke in front.

Pembroke looked across the street, then at Track. "Just what the hell is going on, huh? I get a call from the home office telling me to meet you guys at O'Hare, then do exactly what you say."

"You're doing a good job, too," Track commented.

"Hey, look, what are you guys doing messing with the Vandals. If they wanted to, they could keep me in claims adjusting from now until doomsday just by tearing up this part of town.''

"Relax," Track told him, smiling.

"Relax my—" Then Pembroke glanced in the rearview mirror at Chesterton. He looked at Track. "What now?" The Cadillac was parked across the street from Vandals Enterprises, Inc.

"George and I are going inside. You guys stay in the car."

"What do you plan to do, inside? I mean, take karate lessons or dancing lessons?"

"Neither." Track grinned. "We're going to talk to Rafe Minor."

"Rafe Minor?" Pembroke doubled forward against the steering wheel of the Cadillac, laughing. "Rafe Minor, he—he'll chew you up and eat you for breakfast."

"I say, I don't think talk like that is at all that constructive, Mr. Pembroke," Chesterton interrupted.

Pembroke turned around to face the Englishman. "Mr. Chesterton, I mean Sir Abner, look, Rafe Minor's got his fingers into half the black crime in Chicago and the suburbs. He's got ten thousand members in the gang—"

"Ten thousand?" Track asked. "He must be getting awful selective in his membership these days. But I suppose some of the older guys might have moved or something."

"Ten thousand guys?" George asked.

"Sounds like a fair guess," Track agreed. "That's why he'll be able to help us so much."

"Help you?" Pembroke grinned. "Help you?" His eyebrows raised halfway up his chocolate-colored forehead. "Hey, no offense, huh? But he's not helping three white guys with nothing, Major Track."

Track looked at Chesterton, then back to Pembroke. "You get that major crap from Chesterton, there? Well, just call me Dan."

"Okay, Dan. I just don't want you ending up dead, you dig?"

"Don't worry," Track said. He opened the car door and stepped out onto the sidewalk. Then he leaned back inside. "George, there, has the strength of ten 'cause his heart's pure." Track slammed the door.

George climbed out on the street side. He started walking toward the trunk. They had picked up the guns and other gear at the airport. Track theorized Chesterton had at least bent some laws.

Track walked around to the rear of the car. "No, what we've got on is fine," Track told George.

Track started across the street, the L-Frame S&W in the shoulder rig under his right arm. A Trapper .45 nestled in an Alesai inside the pants holster behind his right hipbone. George carried a Combat Government.

The smell of sweat, garbage, liquor and gasoline assailed the nostrils. There was fear, too. Little kids hawked magazines or listened to transistor radios or tape players. One black child Track judged to be about eight was carrying a twin-speaker cassette tape player on his shoulder. The gleaming machine was nearly as big as he was. The older kids—middle to late teens—hung out along the curb or at the corners.

On the sidewalks there were women, too. Just pretty girls who happened to live in a rough part of town. It was obvious, though, what some of them did for a living.

Track stared at a door three buildings down from Vandals Enterprises. It was open, with music coming from it. An almost painfully thin black girl, a glazed look in her eyes, stood snapping her fingers to the beat of the music. She seemed totally unaware of the bustle on the street around her. Her skirt—too short for normal length, too long for a miniskirt—was tight around her thighs.

"Wonderful part of town you brought me to, Uncle Dan," George observed, lighting a cigarette.

"There's nothing too wrong with this part of town," Track told him, dodging a metallic-gray Cadillac with a cloverleaf-style rear window and a television antenna on the trunk lid. "Most of the people who live here are good decent folk. Probably better churchgoers than you or I could ever be. Just a few rough guys and women."

"I think they all turned out to meet us."

There were three youths standing beside the plate-glass window. The red lettering across the window proclaimed, Vandals Karate Institute, with phone numbers and hours.

Track started for the door. He slowed as the three men—one of them wearing a nylon stocking over his hair, the other two hatless—stepped between Track and the door. "You dudes lookin' for somethin'?"

Track smiled. "You get out of my way, or Rafe Minor's going to be needing a new window and he'll be real mad at you."

"How come?" the stocking-headed man asked.

"'Cause he's going to throw you through it." Track jerked his thumb at George.

"He gonna?" the one wearing a yellow shirt asked.

"Yep, he's tough. He fights a lot. Me, I just shoot

people." Track let his leather jacket swing open to show the L-Frame in the Cobra rig.

"Hey, brother, I'm cool," Yellow Shirt said, laughing.

The other two stepped away while Yellow Shirt did the same.

"Pigs," the one with the nylon on his head snapped.

Track looked at him but said nothing. He passed him by, shouldering the glass door into the karate school, feeling George right behind him.

The floor was covered with green indoor-outdoor carpet. In one corner was a new-looking metal desk behind which a pretty girl sat. A wood-paneled partition ran the width of the room behind her chair.

She cleared her throat. "Can I help you gentlemen?" she asked.

Track walked over to the desk, giving her a big smile. He glanced past the desk to the curtained doorway that led to the larger rear portion of the first floor.

"Yes, I'd like to see Rafe Minor. We used to pal around together when we were younger," Track told her, smiling still. "I've got some important business."

"I'm sorry, but Mr. Minor can't—"

"Can't be disturbed," Track finished for her.

"That's right," she said apologetically.

"Tell him it's Dan Track."

"If you'd like to leave your name and where you can be reached, I'm sure he'll try to get back to you."

"Just tell him I'm here."

"I'm afraid I can't do that."

"Do it, please." Track smiled again.

She pushed a red button next to the telephone on the top of the desk, then stood up, stepping back toward the wall. A buzzer sounded from somewhere inside the karate school behind the wall.

"Now why did you do that?" Track asked her, shaking his head.

Three big men wearing white *gis* and brown belts parted the curtain and stepped through the doorway. They waited, and a moment later a fourth man in black with a black belt also came out. Two of the white-clad men were black; the other one and the man in black were Oriental.

"Hi, guys," Track greeted them. "You're in trouble." He jerked his thumb back toward George. "He's going to kick the crap out of you."

Track looked up. The Oriental in white started past him toward George. Track wheeled half right, his left foot snapping out a fast double Tae Kwon Doe kick to the abdomen and chest. The man staggered back, reeling. He regained his balance and assumed a guard position.

The second Oriental, in the black outfit, was already moving. Track finished the wheeling stance and feigned a kick with his right, landing on the same foot. He backhanded the edge of his left hand into the black-clad Oriental's throat. Before the man had time to fall, Track snapped out three straight-arm punches in rapid succession into the man's face—left, right, left. The guy slammed into the wall, then slid to the floor, unconscious.

Track looked up as the two black men came at him. He lifted one of them up bodily, sidestepping to let the other rush past. Track threw the first one forward. The man's spine crunched against the edge of the metal desk as the girl screamed. Track spun around in time to see

George's left arm rocketing up almost from his toes toward the other black's jaw. The blow sent the man's body jackknifing across the desk as the girl screamed again.

Track balanced on his right foot, his hands in a guard position. He stepped forward on his right foot then, feet apart, the middle knuckles of his right hand snaking out into the first Oriental's face. As the man fell backward, Track rushed forward and leaped into the air, a double drop kick slamming the man against the wall. The man crumpled into an unmoving heap.

Then Track shouted, "Behind you, George!" The three men who had accosted them on the street had just entered the room—Yellow Shirt, Nylon Head and The Silent One.

George did not wait for their attack. He picked up The Silent One and threw him across the room. Track dodged left as the body flew past him. Then George was locked in combat with Nylon Head and Yellow Shirt. George switched to a left-handed fighting stance, snapping out his right. Yellow Shirt dodged left, straight into George's swinging left hand. The blow caught him in the middle of the forehead, knocking him sprawling.

Nylon Head was coming at George, the straight razor he was holding glinting dully in the fluorescent light. The young black dipped left. George moved left and jumped back as the man swiped at him. The blade missed, and George grabbed the man's wrist, jerking his arm behind his back. The man screamed in pain as his arm snapped at the shoulder, and the razor clattered to the floor.

Nylon Head fell back, whimpering as he dashed for the door.

George, out of breath now, turned to Track. "That it?"

Track shrugged, stepping forward, his hands still in a guard position—tucked against his sides, fists curled and out.

"Maybe. Let's go through the opening beyond the partition there. Come on." Track started forward.

They reached the partition simultaneously, and Track stepped back, saying to George, "You first, son."

George looked at him, mimicking, " 'You first, son.' Thanks a hell of a lot." George stepped through, and Track followed. Suddenly George exclaimed, "Oh, no, not again!" Four men in *gis* with white belts were running at them.

"Hey, George, you want all of them? They're just white belts."

"Shut up and give me a hand, Dan," George snarled, letting the nearest of the four men come at him with a flying kick. George just sidestepped it, diving left as the man flew past. Before the man could regain his balance, George whipped out the Colt Combat and blackjacked the man with the pistol's butt.

Track stepped to the right as two of the three remaining attackers approached him. George grabbed the third man by the throat and crotch, lifting him bodily, then throwing him flat against the wall. The wall trembled and fell as the secretary ran through the door screaming.

Track's two opponents were closing on him. He wheeled, pivoting on his left foot. His right caught the first guy in the abdomen, hammering him back. Track wheeled again as the second man punched out a straight-arm right. Track's left foot snapped up and out twice to the right rib cage. The man fell back like a worn-out toy.

Track caught George's eyes. Then they both looked left.

A tall black man with a grin on his face stood at the far end of the practice floor, a pump riot shotgun in his hands. He was laughing. "Fuck, you ain't changed a bit, Dan!"

Track murmured to George. "See, told you he'd be glad to see me!"

21

It had turned cold in the two hours they talked inside the Vandals headquarters. Sir Abner Chesterton had joined them, and Chesterton and Rafe Minor hit it off far better than Track had imagined. Walter Pembroke—the insurance adjuster—was being fed Coca-Cola and hamburgers downstairs in the karate school. The hamburgers were from another Vandals Enterprises subsidiary over on the next block.

Track, George and Chesterton had used the back staircase with Rafe Minor, leaving Walter to finish his feed, then take the rest of the day off. Rafe Minor's white Cadillac was pulling out of the alley as Track and the others hit the street.

Track shivered in the leather bomber jacket against the cold wind.

"The Hawk, man. 'Member The Hawk?" Minor asked Track, grinning.

Track nodded. "Yeah, I remember The Hawk, Rafe."

And Minor laughed.

"The Hawk?" Chesterton asked Minor.

"Yeah, Sir Abner, that's what we call the wind here. You know, Windy City?"

"But why 'The Hawk?' " Chesterton persisted.

Track answered him, " ' 'Cause it swoops down out of

nowhere, cuts through you like two sets of sharp talons and you feel the wound after it leaves.'' Track rolled his eyes at Rafe Minor as Minor grinned.

They saw some sixty-odd men standing outside a huge warehouse.

Track didn't ask who owned the warehouse, and he wasn't about to ask what was inside it. If Rafe Minor wouldn't let them go in, it had to be important enough that asking was dangerous.

So they stood outside, leaning against Rafe Minor's Cadillac. The men were all black except Track, Chesterton and George. None of them was older than Track by much, but some of them were younger than George. They were chieftains of local divisions of the Vandals Street Gang and Athletic Club.

Rafe Minor turned to Track, saying, ''Stand up there on the hood of the Caddy, Dan, it's cool.''

Track only nodded, climbing up onto the hood. It was slippery footing and the hood sagged under him. He looked at Rafe Minor.

Minor shrugged. ''No sweat, Dan.''

Track nodded again.

Rafe—below him—shouted, ''All right, let's be cool. Listen up! Listen!''

Track cleared his throat and began to speak.

''My name's Dan Track. I used to duke it out with a lot of you guys when we were kids. This guy—'' he pointed to George ''—is my nephew, George.''

''Hey, George baby,'' a voice from the back drawled, and someone laughed.

Rafe Minor shouted, ''I said be cool, dammit!''

Track cleared his throat again. ''Okay, the other guy is Sir Abner Chesterton. There's a bad dude running around with some stolen five-hundred-kiloton nuclear warheads.'' Track scanned the faces below him. Many of them looked puzzled, and a few were unimpressed.

''I'll explain how dangerous the situation is,'' Track continued. ''Hiroshima and Nagasaki were leveled during World War II with bombs a lot less than one megaton. The total power of these warheads combined is more than fifty times one megaton in destructive power. This dude's name is Johannes Krieger, and he's a bad mother. He can look like anybody—your brother, your father, your preacher. He can even disguise himself to look like old Rafe here.''

There was laughter, and Track raised his right hand after a moment.

''We think we know his first target—Chicago. We think it might be Stagg Field by the university. The warhead might be set to detonate in the next two minutes, might not be planted yet, might be planted already and set with a timer, or radio detonated. He's got the services of the top terrorist bomber in the world—man named Klaus Gurnheim. They're both Nazis. Maybe Krieger wants to rule the world. Anyway, he's got those warheads, and we figure he's getting ready to pop one off here in Chicago maybe real soon. The cops don't know what we know yet and won't for another twelve hours. That means we can work through until midday tomorrow without blue Mars lights all over the place.''

''What about evacuatin'?'' Rafe Minor asked.

''We thought of that,'' Chesterton answered for Track. ''But to evacuate Chicago if there weren't a warhead here would be needlessly causing death and destruction. If there is a five-hundred-kiloton warhead, it'd be typical of Krieger's mentality, his barbarism, to detonate it where the greatest number of evacuees would be hurt. To clear the city would be impossible without days of work. The cost of human life is too great to gamble.''

"That's good sense, brother," a voice from the back of the crowd shouted.

"The Man would make sure we was the last ones outta town, anyway," somebody else shouted.

Track tried to laugh but couldn't.

When the crowd quieted, Track, his voice tinged with anger, said, "We've got to find Krieger or the team he's using. But finding just one warhead won't stop him. There are other cities, other times. Still, at any cost, we've got to find the warhead he's planting here and deactivate it. Sir Abner's getting me some dope on how to do that, but I don't have it yet. Not the kind of thing Uncle Sam puts out in comic books. I understand the Vandals are down to just ten thousand guys."

Laughter.

"Is that enough of you guys to cover the U of C, cover the whole city? Is it?"

Rafe Minor answered. And it wasn't really an answer. He just seemed to ignore it. "All right, I want the top twelve up here by the car right now. Then subchiefs will get together with their warlord and get briefed out. Now," Rafe shouted, "let's get this mother rollin'!"

22

"Let me help you, Sister," the bus driver said, reaching up his right hand.

Krieger smiled warmly, letting the bus driver take his elbow as he gathered up the long black skirt. "Thank you, young man, and God bless you, too." His voice was that of an old lady. Krieger stopped at the base of the bus steps, looking from side to side at the traffic and the crush of humanity in the Chicago Loop.

Then, gathering his skirts again, he started walking toward the hotel front. He stopped there, waiting, his wrinkled hands folded together at the bodice of the black habit. A gust of wind whipped at the white veil.

The bus driver stopped unloading luggage and called over to him, "Sister, is someone meeting you?"

"Yes, thank you," Krieger replied, assuming the old-lady voice. "Some of the parishioners are coming, young man."

The bus driver smiled and returned to his work. Krieger watched as he moved Sister Mary Genevieve's luggage.

The three suitcases contained the disassembled nuclear warhead.

Krieger stood at the curb. The diesel fumes from the idling bus were making him dizzy. A minute later, a car pulled up next to him.

A man was driving the car with another man next to him. Krieger settled himself in the back next to a blond-haired, chubby woman. Krieger sat behind the front-seat passenger. He kept using the feminine voice until the car was away from the curb.

Then the woman beside him said, "It's amazing, Mr. Krieger. . . that you can do what you do. I mean—"

"The disguises?" Krieger slipped back into his own voice but tried to keep his bodily attitude that of his character's. There was a great deal of traffic, and he had no desire to attract even the slightest suspicion. "I select a character long in advance, either a real character whose identity I must assume or a fictitious character whose identity I can use at any time. Sister Mary Gene-vieve, for example—" and he slipped back into the wavery older feminine voice "—she's such a dear old person."

He reverted to his own voice again, reaching up to the heart-shaped object at the base of the wimpled collar just over his nearly flat-chested breasts. "This, for example, is metal." He touched the cross that hung on the long oversized rosary trailing down the side of his black, ankle-length skirt. "This is metal."

Glancing through the window to see that no pedestrian or motorist might be looking, he raised the black poncholike dress beneath the white collar to show where the sleeves of the dress met the armpit. "These are pinned—again metal." He hiked up his skirt above his knees to expose his right thigh. A razor-blade-thin knife in a sheath was held up by garter clips. "In some respects, it is the perfect disguise." He dropped the skirt again. He was tired of talking to the woman, but had decided to be polite. She was the wife of the Nazi driver.

"But Mr. Krieger," the woman persisted, "I—I just don't know how to— Oh, never mind."

"Do I like women, or just like to dress like them? I disguise myself however is necessary," Krieger told her. "Yesterday I was a general in the United States Army, before that something else. And yes, I like women. Very much." He turned away from the woman beside him, staring into the street.

Wind gusted outside. He could hear and feel it on the exposed skin of his face—even through the makeup—through the partially opened window. There was a tall thin girl standing at the curb, waiting beside a bus-stop sign. The wind caught at her blond hair, and he looked at her closely as the car passed her. "I like women very much," he murmured.

HE SECURED THE DARK TIE with a Windsor knot, then picked up the handcuff tie tack from the dresser. He placed the tack on the tie, securing it to the blue shirt he wore.

Krieger stepped back from the mirror, satisfied with his appearance. He was now dark haired, with a neatly trimmed brush mustache and a scar over his left eyebrow. The gold-capped canine tooth glittered on the right side of his mouth.

He turned away from the mirror and located the gun belt and the handcuff case. The Chicago policeman outfit was perfect. Already at his trouser belt was a S&W Model 36 blue Chiefs Special. He put on the gun belt, then picked up the revolver that lay on the bed—a S&W Model 19. He settled the revolver in the holster after checking the cylinder again. He reached for the officer's cap, not bothering to put it on.

He walked out of the bedroom into the narrow hallway of the South West Side home, then turned right and down the steps, stopping halfway. The blond-haired wife of the Nazi looked up, saying, "It can't be you!"

Jilly Mason, who had come by a different route and arrived three hours before Krieger himself, laughed. "Johannes, you should have stayed an actor. You are brilliant!"

In his new Midwestern voice, blunt, slightly nasal, Krieger said, "You bastards are under arrest. Up against the wall and spread 'em." Then Krieger laughed.

THE BASEMENT RECREATION ROOM—already curtained against the eyes of prying neighbors—had been converted to the bomb factory. The pool table was covered with a floral-print bedsheet, and over that was a plastic painter's drop cloth. Now Krieger was working over the table, following the directions given him by Klaus Gurnheim.

The diameter of the warhead element was eighteen inches—composed of something Gurnheim had called "a rather interesting alloy with titanium elements." There were eighteen "nuclear bits" arranged in a circle along the circumference of the warhead element.

Beyond these and between them and the warhead body was a shaped charge of conventional explosive, forming concentric circles. The "nuclear bits" were shielded in cylindrical lead containers, to prevent radiation leak and to stop the accidental establishment of critical mass during assembly or moving, thus blocking an accidental explosion.

Krieger made the last adjustment to the electronics, then fitted his detonation device. It was ready.

He checked the Timex watch that went with his new

disguise. He watched the sweep second hand, then looked at the diode counter on the detonator shift. He had set both according to the time the telephone operator had given him. He watched the second hand edge past twelve, then flicked the toggle switch on the detonator at the same second. The diode for it matched perfectly with the watch.

"Plutonium," he announced to the Nazi, his pudgy wife, the second Nazi and to Jilly Mason. "A wonderful substance, isn't it?" Then he switched from his own voice to that of the cop. "Hot damn!" Jilly Mason was the only one who laughed.

"HOW CAN YOU just sit there so calmly, Mr. Krieger?" asked Belcher, the husband of the blond woman.

Krieger was relaxing in an overstuffed armchair in the Belchers' living room, sipping his coffee. Jilly Mason reclined on the sofa.

In his own voice Krieger answered, "Very easily. The bomb will not detonate until it is supposed to detonate. It is totally safe."

"I've been a Nazi for fifteen years, but I never did anything like this," the man said.

Krieger smiled at him and then at the second Nazi. "But you have been loyal to the party—more than that, to the ideal. Anyone can go out wearing a swastika armband and picket a synagogue, or pick fights with blacks. But you have done none of that."

"My father, his brother—they both served the führer."

"And served him well in the underground here—as you serve the new order that will come because of your efforts."

"Mr. Krieger, would it not be possible," Mr. Belcher

asked, "to know your true identity? It would mean a lot to my wife, Janet. And I could tell our grandchildren that we knew you, were here when the new order began."

Krieger smiled expansively. "Perhaps this is my real face. Perhaps I am really that old nun or perhaps someone else. If you do not know me as I really am, then you are in no danger—"

"That we might betray you?" the second Nazi asked.

Krieger sipped again at his coffee. "Mrs. Belcher, you make excellent coffee," he told the blond woman.

She smiled, then said, "Is that it, then, Mr. Krieger? That we might accidentally betray you?"

Krieger laughed. "I trust your loyalties. Only drugs or the most severe tortures might force you to denounce your vows. But, no, it is for your safety. As long as you do not know me, you cannot be cruelly abused by the Americans into divulging that which you do not know. It is for your safety, not mine, that I hide my face."

"But—" It was the blond woman.

Krieger looked at the Timex. There was still time to talk. "Yes, Frau Belcher?"

She smiled at his use of the word *Frau*. "I just wondered...ahh...with your...your personal life—"

He interrupted her. "If I take a woman, I wear my own face. But since no one knows the face of Johannes Krieger, it does no harm. Does that—" and he smiled "—answer your question, Frau Belcher?"

Her husband turned to her. "Janet, that's enough! You're embarrassing Mr. Krieger."

"Yes. Yes, William," she answered dutifully, looking down at her hands in her lap.

Krieger coughed, then said, "The other four will be here shortly, correct?"

"Yes," the second Nazi replied.

"Then we will proceed to the university, deposit the device and radio detonate after we are safely away."

"But the timer?" Mrs. Belcher asked.

"The timer is a backup system," Krieger told her easily, smiling. "In the event of our capture, I can use the radio device to lock into the timer and either disarm the system remotely or trigger it within five minutes." He lit a cigarette.

"While Mrs. Belcher goes to safety," he continued, "we seven will plant the device. Jilly will be waiting to airlift us." He glanced at his watch, then at Jilly Mason. "Jilly, take Mrs. Belcher to the others who are loyal and travel to safety."

"Yes, Johannes," Jilly Mason said, uncoiling himself from the sofa, smiling at Janet Belcher.

She stood up, fussing with her clothes for an instant. Then she leaned down and hugged her husband's neck. "William, be careful," she murmured. She looked at all of them collectively, then individually. "Mr. Krieger, bless you." And then to the second Nazi, "And bless you, too, Fred."

"Thanks, Janet," Fred said. "We'll be fine." Then he laughed. "I'll bring Bill safely back home to you."

She sniffed once loudly, then started from the room. Jilly Mason, riveting his eyes for an instant to Krieger's, followed her out of the room.

23

Track looked out from the second floor of Vandals Enterprises, Inc. down onto Forty-seventh Street. He said into the telephone, "Yes, that's right, Tassles, nothing new to type." He nodded into the receiver. "Right, and I'm almost out of cat food for Dorothy. So get some up there if you can, right." He nodded again. "You handle the insurance adjuster. If he's got a gripe I'm not there, call me." He read her the number from Rafe Minor's private line. "But don't give the number to anybody else, particularly the FBI.

"Yes, I know Miles Jefferson...honest man, good agent. He hates my guts. Don't tell him a thing, but learn how you can get in contact with him. Okay?" He nodded into the receiver once more. "Nobody does it like you, doll. Take care, Tassles." He hung up.

George, standing beside the window, asked, "Who's Tassles?"

Track looked up. "Didn't I tell you about Tassles LaToure?"

"No," George answered.

"Yes, the stripper."

"A stripper?"

Track nodded, smiling. "*The* Tassles LaToure. She quit stripping a while back—just got tired of taking off her clothes every night. Been my secretary for a year and half. You'll meet her sometime.''

"Hey," George began, his eyes glinting. "What about—ah—"

"You want me to introduce you to her, you mean," Track concluded.

"Well—" George hedged.

"You want me to set you up, then?" Track wanted to know.

"What do you mean, 'set me up'?"

"A date?"

"Hey, Dan, I don't want to cut in."

Track smiled, gesturing with his hands, shrugging. "There's never been anything between Tassles and me. Not a thing that isn't professional. But she's a hell of a nice lady, if you know what I mean." Track winked.

"Could you, I mean, maybe I could take her out to dinner or something, you know?"

"Wait till we get back to New Mexico," Track said, grinning. "I'll take care of it. Look, you're my nephew, so nothing's too good for you, okay?"

"Thanks, Dan." George nodded, smiling.

Track just grinned.

Chesterton and Rafe Minor came through the door into Minor's office. "Beautiful view, huh?" Minor asked.

Track glanced back down at Forty-seventh Street. "Oh, yeah, really."

Chesterton sat in one of the leather armchairs beside the desk and pushed his feet out of his loafers, wiggling his toes. Minor went around the desk and sank into the leather swivel chair. "So you make your phone call?"

"Yes, got my secretary to look after the cat—all set. How about you?"

"Guys are reportin' in already from the university, the campus. And from all over the South Side. Nothin', man. Big fat zero."

"But I came up with something enormously useful," Chesterton cut in.

Track looked at him, watching the grin on the older man's face.

Chesterton looked at George. "And it's thanks to you, dear boy."

"Me?"

"Yes, definitely you," Chesterton said.

Track stood up, watching Chesterton dig into his pockets. Track got a glimpse of the Bianchi shoulder rig with the stainless Walther PPK American that Chesterton now wore.

Chesterton stopped fumbling in his pockets and produced a leather notebook and a gold pen. He tapped at the note page as he started to read, "According to George H. Beegh, description of General Fleyderman's pilot, hmm?" And he looked up, smiling at George, then at Track, then at Rafe Minor. "First of all," Chesterton began, "a friend in Army CID—"

Track laughed. It was a mutual friend.

"—revealed that General Fleyderman is presumed dead. Fingerprints found on the scene of the helicopter thefts were distinct enough to indicate they were not Fleyderman's, not a single half a thumbprint. Fleyderman's house showed signs of illegal entry. Fleyderman's wife is missing, but their bank accounts—none of that has been touched. This morning George gave me a description of the pilot. The man was slightly built, blond haired, smiled a good deal and seemed, well—''

"I said he looked like a homosexual, the expression in his eyes, the way he moved. He just seemed—well, I don't.''

"Going on the assumption that you're right, George," Chesterton continued, "I checked for a blond-haired, slightly built homosexual helicopter pilot with a Vietnam war record. I came up with just one man—a crack helicopter pilot. A known terrorist since those days. In and out of jail. Wanted currently for ice-picking somebody in San Francisco. Also, for his involvement in a brawl just recently there, too, with a tall effeminate-looking but muscular man who fought like a martial-arts expert.''

"Krieger," whispered Track.

"My thought, exactly, Dan," Chesterton said. "Man's name is Jilly Mason. He worked with Krieger before, we think.''

"If Krieger is plantin' a damn bomb. . . ." Rafe Minor remarked. "Hell, I was in demolitions in Nam up near the DMZ. You can blow up anythin' with anythin', but the trick of the thing is not to be there when the mother goes.''

"So Krieger would have the same problem, only on a bigger scale," Track murmured.

"So he'd need a helicopter," George added.

"He'd need the best and most reliable helicopter pilot he could find. Someone totally ruthless and totally loyal to him," Chesterton added.

"That fag guy," Minor said.

"Jilly Mason," Chesterton added. "Born Jessup Aloysius Mason here in the Midwest, in Davenport, Iowa," Chesterton read from his pad. "For a time he worked as a helicopter pilot after the war—here in Chicago, at a place called Midway Airport. The ownership of the helicopter service has changed twice since then, but—''

"Holy shit," Minor rasped, grabbing up his telephone, punching the comline button. "This is Rafe. Get my wheels in the alley in sixty seconds, quick!" Then he hung up.

Track snapped the Metalife Custom out from the Cobra rig, checked the cylinder and holstered it as he went through the door behind Minor, Chesterton and George.

24

The gray van stopped at the corner, turning right onto Ninety-fifth Street and heading east. William Belcher was driving. Krieger, wearing a Windbreaker over his Chicago-police-uniform shirt and his hat on his lap, sat beside him. In the back of the van were Fred and four other men. Krieger looked out over the short sloping hood along the street. "We are in Oak Lawn still?" he asked.

"Yes, Mr. Krieger," Belcher answered.

"Have all key personnel, with the exception of yourselves, been removed a safe distance from Chicago?"

"Yes, Mr. Krieger," Belcher answered.

"You are brave men. Your names will be revered by future generations," Krieger told them. He knew it was what they wanted to hear.

No one said anything.

Krieger checked his map; there were no notations written on it. He memorized notations, rather than leaving them as evidence. "You plan to turn left on Western Avenue to Seventy-ninth Street, then proceed east again toward the university and Stagg Field?"

"Yes, Mr. Krieger," Belcher said. Krieger was watching him.

"Good, but when we near Western Avenue, please inform me."

Belcher looked at him. "Yes, sir."

Several minutes passed without anyone saying anything. Then Belcher broke the silence. "Sir, this is California Street. Western is four long blocks ahead."

"Very good," Krieger said, glancing up from his map. "There is a different plan. I saved its detail until the last minute. You will turn right instead and proceed to the end of the line station for what I believe is called the Lake Street Elevated."

"The L?" Fred asked from behind him.

"Yes," Krieger droned in his own voice. "The bomb will not be detonated at the university as I indicated. The last-minute change is for security purposes only. In the event of a leak—"

"Surely none of us—" Belcher almost pleaded.

"Of course not," Krieger reassured him. "But there are others who might possibly have unwittingly divulged some tidbit of information that even now the FBI or some other organization might be acting upon. We shall plant the bomb on the elevated train, and it shall be left aboard the train at the far Western station just past the suburb of Oak Park. I believe the place is Harlem Avenue?"

"Yes, sir," Belcher said.

"The bomb will be detonated there in the switching yard. The six of you will accompany it to make certain it remains secure. Once you leave the bomb, I would have you open the bomb case and flick the toggle switch marked *A*." He glanced back toward the trunk-sized suitcase between the five men who sat in the rear of the van.

"After working this toggle switch," Krieger proceeded, "you will have exactly one half hour to reach a forest preserve located near First Avenue and North Avenue, not far from the switching yard. Jilly Mason will be waiting for you with a helicopter.''

The van made the right-hand turn onto Western Avenue. Krieger stripped off his Windbreaker and put on his police-officer's hat. "I wish you good luck," he said in his own voice, then added in the character of the Chicago policeman, "I'm countin' on you guys a hell of a lot."

Belcher only nodded.

25

The sign read, Windy City Choppers—Executive Helicopter Service—Flight Instruction Available.

Track stepped out of Rafe Minor's Cadillac, following Chesterton. George and Rafe Minor were already walking toward the doorway of the chopper-service office. A second car pulled up behind them, and four of Rafe Minor's men exited the car. It was a Fleetwood, several years old but in excellent condition. Track guessed it was armor plated.

Track saw George and Minor returning with a third man between them.

"This dude says he rented out his last charter about fifteen minutes ago," Rafe said.

Track looked at Minor, then past him at a blue-and-white Bell 206L Long Ranger helicopter. "What the hell's that, a mirage?" Track shouted.

"No, but I don't have another pilot, mister," the man between Rafe Minor and George shouted.

Track walked up to him. "Who did you rent it to?"

"None of your—"

Track reached under his coat and pulled the Metalife L-Frame, thumb-cocking the hammer and resting the muzzle against the tip of the man's nose. "I don't mean to be unfriendly, but the guy you rented it to—was he blond, kind of slight? Maybe looked like he was gay?"

Track didn't move the muzzle of the revolver; the man stared at it cross-eyed. "Yeah, that was him. He said he had to pick up a half-dozen guys out in the western suburbs and bring 'em back here. That's his car over there." The man's eyes uncrossed as they flickered to Track's left.

Track glanced that way. A green Ford LTD was parked by a small, abandoned-looking hangar.

Rafe Minor was already calling to the men beside the armored-plated Fleetwood. "Buster, Floyd, you other two, go can-opener that Ford."

"Watch out for fingerprints—the ones already on the car," Track called after them. Then he looked back at the proprietor of the helicopter service. The brown eyes were still crossed on the muzzle of the gun. Track shifted the muzzle away and lowered the hammer.

The man breathed audibly. "You guys cops?"

"Western suburbs," Track repeated, ignoring the man's question.

"Uh-huh, that's what the blond guy said."

"I want to rent the chopper you have there. She fueled and checked out?"

The man nodded. "But it won't do you any good. My other pilot's out with the third helicopter."

"I can fly a helicopter," Track told him. "Haven't been up in one for more than a year, but it's like riding a bicycle. Comes back to you."

"Hey, ain't no way nobody's flyin' one of—"

Track pulled the L-Frame again, thumb-cocking it, resting it on the tip of the man's nose again. "Now I wouldn't shoot you, but these guys—" he nodded toward George and Rafe Minor "—will probably rip your arms off and beat you to death."

"I'll get the keys," the man stammered.

"Hey, Rafe!"

Track looked left. It was one of Rafe's men, standing beside the green Ford; the trunk lid was open.

"George," Track snapped. "Get our friend to start up the motors if he can. Hurry." Track lowered the L-Frame's hammer and started after Rafe, running toward the rented car beside the old hangar.

"Man!" Minor exclaimed as Track stopped beside the trunk next to Minor. Through a rip in a couple of green plastic trash can liners he could see part of a woman's face and some blond hair. The face was a little chubby. The eyes were wide open, glassy. The shaft of an ice pick was poking out of her jugular vein.

"Jilly Mason," Track whispered.

"That mother—" Rafe let it hang.

26

"Hey, pilot," Jilly Mason called out, tapping the thin, dark-haired man on the shoulder.

"Yeah?" the pilot shouted back over the twin-blade rotor noise.

"We're going south now," Jilly shouted.

"What? Thought we were heading out to the western suburbs," the pilot shouted back.

Jilly looked down at the streets below them. "No, everybody, at least anybody who's interested, should think that by now. No use not telling you, though," Jilly said. "I'm taking the helicopter to the far South Side. Picking up only one man, not six. Those six other men—they're carrying a nuclear warhead aboard one of your L trains. They think it won't go off for a half hour after they set the timer, but it's just a fake timer," he shouted. "The real timer—" he glanced at his watch "—was set two minutes ago. The warhead will detonate just as the L train passes through downtown Chicago— the early rush hour. Poof, all gone. Five-hundred kilotons' worth."

The pilot started to reach for him, but Jilly jabbed the Browning's muzzle against the pilot's rib cage. He pumped the trigger three times, then reached out and grabbed the controls. He released the pilot's seat belt, then reached across and flicked open the door-handle latch, letting the door swing out against the slipstream around them. He gave the dead pilot a shove. If he wasn't dead, Jilly reasoned, he would be by the time he landed in the vacant lot below them.

The body fell away from the hovering chopper.

Jilly watched, fascinated, as the body tumbled downward. It was so graceful. He had been a nice-looking man. "Poof, all gone." Jilly sighed wistfully.

27

George had the two M-16s with the Aimpoint sights. The guns rested between George's legs, with the muzzle caps still in place. George, Chesterton, Floyd and Buster were in the back of the chopper, while Rafe Minor sat up front beside Track.

Minor had a Mossberg 500ATP6P riot shotgun. Each of his two men, Floyd and Buster, had H&K 93s in .223. Chesterton had a SPAS 12 across his lap.

Minor was tuning the Bearcat scanning monitor set under the helicopter instrument panel, trying to pick up police frequencies. Chicago police, he explained, broadcast on one frequency and received on another.

The scanning monitor crackled, then a voice came on. It was a district-headquarters bulletin. "All units in the vicinity of Seventy-ninth and Kostner...citizen report of a body-shaped object being thrown from a helicopter, landing in vacant lot. This is a—"

Minor cut off the monitor. "Jilly Mason?" he shouted to Track.

"Jilly Mason!" Track shouted back, then added over his shoulder, "George, get one of those M-16s ready to go. Don't forget the muzzle cap. Those things cost money to replace when you shoot them off."

"No kidding!"

Track laughed, banking the Bell Long Ranger hard starboard, pouring on speed.

In the distance, through the industrial pollution and smoke, he saw something. He poured on more speed, glancing through the clear panels beneath his feet, seeing blue-and-white squad cars converging on a vacant lot below him. A dark twisted shape lay in the center of the lot. The shape was obscured by dust as the police cars closed in. The object ahead of him in the sky grew clearer now—a helicopter. He pushed the speedometer over ninety, going after it.

"All right, asshole," Track growled. He only wished Jilly Mason could hear him.

28

Krieger walked along the platform. His men were long gone aboard the train now; the timer was set. All was in readiness. He saw a young black man trying to steal the purse off an older black woman. True to his role, Krieger started toward them, shouldering the young black man aside. "Get outta here before you wind up in the slammer, kid," he snarled. The young man's eyes were angry black dots, with yellow where the whites should be. Krieger guessed that he used drugs.

"Hey, man, I'm not doin' nothin', so be cool, Officer, huh?"

Krieger smiled, glancing from left to right. No one was watching yet. He rammed his knee into the young black's crotch. The kid doubled toward him. Krieger grabbed him, asking in a louder-than-normal voice, "Hey, you all right, kid? Want me to call an ambulance?" Then he shoved the young man back against a pillar that supported the roof over the train platform.

"Nah, but you ain't seen the last of me, man," said the young black, starting to run across the platform.

Krieger turned to the older black woman, tapping his right index finger to the brim of his cap like a salute. "Everything okay, ma'am?"

"Thank you, Officer. I'm all right now," she said.

He gave her his best police-officer grin and continued

along the platform. In the distance he heard the whirring beat of rotor blades. He looked up and saw the helicopter closing in. It would be Jilly Mason. He started down toward the parking lot, walking quickly.

The helicopter was coming in fast, hovering, gliding downward now into an open area between parked cars.

Krieger started to run toward it, holding the butt of the revolver in the hip holster. The chopper was less than ten yards away now. He could see Jilly switching seats in the chopper. He could hear him shout as Krieger narrowed the distance to five yards. "Johannes, there's somebody after me!"

The voice was a pleading bleat, like a whining child asking for help.

Krieger stared at Mason for an instant, then looked skyward. Another helicopter was closing in rapidly.

Krieger started to draw his service revolver. Kill Mason and leave no leads? He hesitated. Leave Mason alive and the occupants of the helicopter would be busy chasing Jilly instead of him.

He smiled broadly, shouting, "Get out of here quickly!" He turned, pushing past the crowd that started to ring itself around the chopper. Suddenly he felt something jab into his left side, burning him, tearing the flesh.

Krieger shouted in pain, stumbling to his knees, falling, turning his head. He saw the young black he had hassled on the train platform, a cheap-looking switchblade in his right hand.

"Honkie mother!" the kid shouted.

Krieger stared, then drew the Model 19 and emptied half the cylinder into the young black's torso. Screams punctuated each shot as the body lurched back off the platform onto the tracks.

Krieger struggled to his feet, his left hand clamped over his left side, his right hand holstering the gun.

He began to run. There was a pain, a swimming feeling in his head, but he ran fast. He had looked at his Timex watch a few moments earlier, and he always judged time well. The bomb would detonate in twenty-seven minutes.

He ran faster.

29

George undid his seat restraint, handing both of the M-16s to Chesterton, snapping, "Here, hold these!" He zigzagged on his feet, moving forward, positioning himself between and behind Dan Track and Rafe Minor. As the helicopter moved wildly downward and ahead, he supported himself by holding on to the seat backs. "What are you doing?"

Track shouted back to him, "Trying to keep that son of a bitch down on the ground!"

George's stomach churned as the helicopter dropped suddenly. George swayed violently left, but he held on, keeping his balance. He looked down now through the transparent panel in front of their feet. The Bell 206L seemed to hover just a few feet above the chopper skimming the surface below them. The parking lot was jammed with cars. The helicopter below threaded its way through the open lanes. Track kept the other chopper down by hovering almost directly over it.

There was a howling wind rushing around them. The chopper zigzagged again. George lost his balance, and slammed against the bulkhead.

"Sit down, dammit, George!" Track shouted.

"You'll never get him this way, Dan!" George shouted over the wind and the downdraft.

The helicopter below them cut right suddenly. George

almost lost his balance again as the floor spun beneath him. Below, the yellow-and-white helicopter was moving fast now, but Track moved faster, stopping the aircraft from rising. The yellow machine started toward the fence line, then spun one hundred eighty degrees. A storm of dust blew along the ground. Track chased it, keeping the Bell's runners a safe distance above the yellow machine's rotor blades.

"I'm going down after him, Dan!" George shouted.

"No!"

"Hell, yes, I am," George shouted, wrenching the door handle on the port side. He pushed the door toward the fuselage nose, holding himself in the doorframe, then waited. The yellow helicopter under George's feet turned violently, heading back toward the fence line of the parking lot.

George spotted a Mercedes 450SL convertible, the top up. He jumped, his track-shod feet impacting against the convertible top. He crashed through it, his arms going out to brace himself. The top shredded under his weight as he fell forward, catching himself across the passenger seat. He pushed himself up and climbed out of the Mercedes.

The yellow helicopter was turning, boxed in from above by the blue-and-white Long Ranger. It did another one-eighty and started toward him. George jumped aside, throwing himself onto the hood of a Chevrolet, then getting to his feet and climbing to the roof. He jumped across to a vinyl-topped Ford parked beside it. The helicopter's runners were less than a yard from him now. He launched himself upward, reaching out. His fingers curled over the yellow-and-white chopper's runners, then locked on them as his feet crashed against the windshield of the Ford.

The chopper pulled up and left. The downdraft from the rotor blades beat at him, whipping his hair across his forehead, tearing at his rolled-up shirt-sleeves, hammering his flesh.

He swung his legs up. Only his left leg caught the runner at his ankle. He pushed forward and over. The runner was under his knee joint now.

He got his left hand free, threw his arm over the runner and hooked his left elbow over it. He looked up, squinting against the wind. He stared at the yellow-and-white helicopter's fuselage for an instant. The pilot's door was open... slapping back and forth.

George reached out with his right hand, getting his elbow over the runner. He moved his left arm forward, catching the forward support strut of the runner. Extending his right hand, he grabbed the door latch. He pulled on it, at the same time pushing up with his left hand on the support strut. Inch by agonizing inch his body slowly rose, buffeted by the downdraft and the wildly gyrating aircraft. He got his left leg under him in an awkward kneeling position. Then he placed his right foot on the strut and pushed himself slowly upright. Both feet were now on the strut. His right hand still grasped the handle, his left was pressed flat against the door, edging for the joint between the door and the fuselage.

George moved forward, his right hand on the door handle, his left arm extended into the doorframe of the pilot's door. The door banged shut against his fingers as the chopper angled hard to port in another one-eighty. He bit the inside of his cheek to keep from screaming.

"Son of a—" he swore. His fingers could still move, but he knew they'd be stiff soon. He could see them, part of the flesh gouged away, bleeding.

Still edging forward, he could look into the chopper now. The blond-haired man sat at the controls, hair blowing in the downdraft. His face was set, a wild hunted look in his eyes as they locked with George's.

Jilly Mason.

The man held an automatic pistol. George heard a shot and his left upper arm burned suddenly, but the pain did not make him loosen his grip.

George's pistol was in the holster on the right hip, he couldn't get to it.

The trapped helicopter wheeled one hundred eighty degrees again, lurching downward, then shooting upward, then leveling off again. The pilot was trying to shake him off. The pistol was tracking back toward him.

George wrenched his body forward with the remaining strength in his left arm as his right leg found the corner of the doorframe. Leaning on the door, he finally threw himself toward Jilly Mason into the cockpit. The pistol discharged into the transparent panel in the floor, sending a rush of air hissing into the cabin. The panel cracked as George's left fist locked over the autoloading pistol Mason held.

George's right snapped out, but he restrained himself. If he killed, crippled or knocked Jilly Mason unconscious, the helicopter would crash.

He slapped out with his right instead, hard across Mason's mouth; the pistol discharged again. George swatted his left down hard onto the pistol and the gun flew out of Mason's hand. Then he snapped the right wrist back against the control panel. The helicopter was lurching violently and a droning whistle starting; the rotor sound overheard was uneven.

George clenched both hands over Mason's throat. Mason was trying to wrench free. "Now, you son of a bitch, land this sucker!" George snarled, lifting Mason out of the pilot's seat by the throat, tensioning him against the seat restraint.

There was a gurgling sound, then a cough. "Yes, all right, yes—don't kill me, please!"

George raised his bloodied left fist from Jilly Mason's throat, backhanding him across the mouth. "You chicken shit!" He looked forward at the controls as Mason's hands worked them. "You crash this thing and you'll be dead before it hits the ground!"

His right hand held Mason's throat tight. His left hand was stiffening, and his left shirt-sleeve was dark and wet with his blood.

30

Track jumped from behind the controls, almost slipping as he hit the parking-lot surface. The downdraft of the twin rotor blades whipped up his hair as he ran toward the yellow-and-white chopper, his L-Frame .357 in his right hand. George was dragging a slightly built, blond-haired man from behind the controls of the aircraft. George's left arm was drenched in blood; his right was clamped around the man's throat.

"What the hell happened to you?" Track shouted over the noise of the throbbing choppers, screams and police sirens in the background.

"Son of a bitch shot me." George grabbed Jilly Mason by the throat, making him cough. "Now tell them what you told me," George shouted to Mason, shaking him by the neck again.

"It won't do you any good. The bomb's on one of the L trains. It left about twelve or fifteen minutes ago...timer's set to go off when it hits the Loop... right in the middle of downtown."

Track pulled back his bomber-jacket's storm sleeve, looking at the Rolex. "Hell!" he snarled.

"Won't do you any good," Mason said again. "Six guys on board—they think it's goin' off with a timer switch they'll set when they hit the end of the line just past Oak Park. But it won't. It'll go off and take them with it!''

Track growled, "Hold him, George." And he was already running, firing the gun in the air to disperse the crowd of curious onlookers blocking his way to the yard house. It was at the far end of the parking lot. Rafe Minor was running beside him. Track emptied the cylinder of the revolver into the air to disperse more of the throng.

"What the hell's going on?" Minor asked.

"Bomb...set to blow in the Loop...in fifteen minutes or so...six guys guarding it on an L train. Come on!" He kept running, hearing Rafe Minor shouting something but not bothering really to listen. Track had to get the number of that train; they left every few minutes.

Police cars were converging on the area as he reached the end of the parking lot. Track scaled a chest-height chainlink fence, snagging his blue jeans on it. He caught his balance as he ripped free, half stumbling toward the steps leading up to the switch house. On the way up he rammed the .357 into his waistband, grabbing the Trapper Scorpion .45 from the inside-the-pants holster behind his right hip.

He reached the top of the steps and tried the switch-house door. It was locked. Two men were inside, one on the phone, both looking frightened. Track took a half step back, then forward, his left foot punching through the glass in the door. He reached his hand through the hole in the glass and twisted the knob, then threw the door open.

He stepped in, glass crunching under his penny-loafered feet. He jabbed the satin nickeled Trapper .45

forward, his right thumb sweeping down the safety, the muzzle aimed at the head of the man on the telephone. "We're the good guys. . .so help us out. . .now! Get on the radio to the train that left here about fifteen minutes ago. . .stop them. There's a nuclear weapon on board set to go off in less than fifteen minutes. . .right in the middle of downtown. Now move!"

The man dropped the receiver. A voice still came scratchily off the line. Track replaced the swinging receiver on its cradle.

The man was at the radio set. "This is South switch-yard. . .calling train forty-one twenty-seven. . .come back—"

There wasn't any answer for a moment.

"This is forty-one twenty-seven. What's shakin', Bob?"

"Some guys here claim they got a bomb on board your train. . .set to blow in the Loop. Nuclear bomb, they say—"

The voice came over the speaker, "Hey, Bob, what the hell you guys—"

The voice went dead—static.

Track grabbed the microphone in his left fist, ramming down the talk button. "Hey, whoever it is on the train. . .you six guys. . .you've been screwed by Krieger. He's killing you, too. The bomb's set to go off when you hit the Loop. Your timer's a fake. . .Jilly Mason told us. . .come in— Hey, come in, for God's sake—"

Nothing.

"For Christ's sake, guys. . .a nuclear weapon. . . you'll kill millions, even yourselves. For Christ's sake—"

Nothing.

"All those people," he said, staring at the muzzle of his pistol.

He looked at Rafe Minor, the riot shotgun trained on both men.

Track closed his eyes, shaking his head to clear it, to think. He looked up at the man who had used the radio. "Bob, is that your name?"

"Yes, Bob Argenfeld—"

Right," Track said. "Bob, get back to the cops. Tell them what's happening. Tell them to stop the train even if they have to derail it. The bomb shouldn't go off from concussion like that, I don't think.... Hell, I don't know...tell them to do something. Something—"

"It would go off that way," Minor said soberly, all the usual bravado of his voice gone. "Remember, I was a demolitions man in Nam. Part of my training was in nuclear arms. It'd go off sky-high."

"Then tell them not to derail it, but tell them to do something," he said to Bob, repeating the number of the train. "Forty-one twenty-seven—right?"

"Right," Bob confirmed, sweating, his face white. "I really believe you, hell!"

Track turned to Rafe Minor. "We take one chopper, you, me, George and Jilly Mason. We'll leave Chesterton with Floyd and Buster to explain it."

Sirens were loud now; through the glass of the switch house blue lights appeared to be everywhere. "What about the cops?"

"Do anything short of killing them. But we must get to the blue-and-white chopper. Come on." Track started for the door, holstering the Trapper .45. He drew the L-Frame .357 Smith out of his waistband, opening the cylinder and dumping the spent shells on the steps. He fitted a Safariland Speed Loader to the cylinder and reloaded, closed the cylinder of the revolver. He held the gun tight in his right hand now.

With Rafe Minor beside him, he started to run. Chicago police were racing toward them, shouting, "Police, freeze!"

The nearest police officer, a revolver in his right hand, started for him. Track wheeled half right, his left foot snaking out in a double Tae Kwon Doe kick to the chest, hammering the man back against two more officers.

Someone shot at him. The slug ricocheted off pavement near his feet. Track reached into the crowd, grabbing a pretty blond girl. The girl screamed as Track pulled her in front of him. Track whispered to her. "Wouldn't hurt you for the world, honey." Then he shouted, "Shoot at me, you have to shoot through her. There's a nuclear warhead on train forty-one twenty-seven...take that yellow-and-white chopper up and follow us if you want to, but help us stop it!"

"Surrender!" a police officer yelled, edging toward them, gun drawn.

Track put the muzzle of the L-Frame to the girl's right temple. "Relax, kid. Just for show," he whispered. Then he shouted, "I'll blow her fucking brains out!"

The cop drew back a half step, lowering the muzzle of his revolver. "The chopper's right behind you," Rafe Minor said.

Track nodded, his eyes never wavering from the crowd, "Sir Abner?"

"Right here, Dan," came Chesteron's voice from behind.

"Get George, Jilly Mason...better add Floyd or Buster, too. George looked like he was losing blood fast. Get them on the blue-and-white chopper and cover us while we get airborne. Let the girl here go and apologize. Give her my phone number, maybe. Then straighten this out with the cops. The train is forty-one twenty-seven. We're going after it...try to stop the bombers and disarm the weapon."

"But how—"

"Let you know when I figure it out myself," Track snapped, laughing. Track ticked off thirty seconds in his head.

"All right, they're aboard. Buster and I are staying behind," Chesterton shouted, and Track wheeled, throwing the girl toward Buster.

Buster's H&K P-7 pistol went to the girl's head.

Track, his .357 still on the crowd and the cops, edged toward the chopper. Rafe was climbing aboard, visible out of his left peripheral vision.

Then Track jumped aboard, ramming the revolver into his waistband. He sat at the controls and revved the Allison engine and started to lift off. The police were closing in; Buster snapped a shot into the air. The police stopped in unison as the gun went back to the blond girl's head.

"We standardized on H-K," Rafe shouted over the whir of the rotors.

Track just looked at him, nodding, his eyes wide.

"What the hell are we doing?" George asked.

Track did not glance over at him. He was busy banking the chopper steeply as he picked up the Dan Ryan Expressway beneath him. On the L tracks running down the center, he saw a train.

"Well?" George's voice demanded.

"Rafe and I have to get on that train, get inside—" Track craned his neck to look at Jilly Mason. "Okay, Jilly, I hear you're one of the best helicopter pilots there is. Well, now's the time to do your stuff. You have to get this thing steady enough that we can climb down, then fly it up and away and follow us."

"Like hell!" Jilly snarled.

"If you don't do exactly as I say, we'll die when that weapon blows, so George here won't have anything to lose. Even with one arm out of commission he'll rip you apart, dismember you, gouge your eyes out, the whole nine yards, Jilly. And in case George gets tired, Floyd there'll help him."

"Right on," Floyd grunted.

Track smiled. "So, you going to cooperate or get your head twisted off?"

He glanced back at Jilly, whose eyes gave the answer.

"Good boy, Jilly. Maybe you'll get off with fifty or sixty consecutive life sentences for helping us out, who knows."

Track started dropping his altitude, skimming over the traffic now in the Loop-bound lanes, trying to read the number on the train as he passed it. The lead car's number panel showed something besides forty-one twenty-seven. He gunned the aircraft, climbing, heading over the tracks again.

"Remember, Jilly," Track shouted, seeing the next train ahead of them. "Do exactly as I say. Then when I'm gone, do what George there says."

"Can I rip him apart now, Uncle Dan, huh?" George asked.

"Not yet," Track laughed, bringing the chopper

down again over the in-bound lanes of the Ryan. He skimmed the traffic trying to see the lead car.

Then Rafe Minor spoke. "That's it, Dan! Forty-one twenty-seven."

"Great," Track rasped. "Get Jilly down here." To his right he saw Jilly Mason and Floyd changing places. "Okay, I'm giving you the controls at the count of three. Fly well, Jilly, for your sake." The chopper climbed and dropped as Jilly Mason took over. "Getting the feel of it?" Track asked.

"Right," Mason said, looking at him a moment, saying nothing else.

"Get us over the train, wherever you can. Watch for the power cables that run near the tracks."

"I've done tougher than this," Mason snarled.

Track unbuckled his seat restraint, turning to Mason standing behind him. "Rafe, take an AR-15. Selective fire might be better. Anyway, no sling on your pump shotgun."

"Right."

Track snatched up a SPAS 12, adjusted the sling, getting it across his back. He hefted it, then swung the shotgun forward, chambering the first round out of the tube, double O buck. It was loaded alternately with buck and hollowpoint.

He moved toward the pilot door, looking at Jilly. "I'm ready when you are." Then Track glanced at his watch—they had about ten minutes left.

"That thing's going damn fast," Rafe shouted over the slipstream. Both the pilot's side door and the passenger door were open slightly, and the wind whistled loudly through the cockpit.

The train was approaching a station. The helicopter

was closing in now. The red warning lights on the track flashed to stop the train, but it was neither stopping nor slowing.

"They're panicking, trying to get to the end of the line near Oak Park as fast as they can!" Track shouted.

The helicopter dropped, skimming perhaps twenty feet over the roof of the train. Jilly Mason shouted, "I'm settling over the lead car, then matching my speed so I can drop you on the roof of the last car. Best I can do!"

Track looked at him, nodding.

The helicopter was going in. The lead car was beneath them now. Track stepped out onto the runner, holding on to the doorframe. The door fought him as the slipstream tried to push it closed. He could see only Rafe Minor's lower legs and feet—the door for the passenger ingress blocked the rest of his body.

Jilly Mason expertly avoided the high tension lines flanking them as he slowed the helicopter to match the speed of the train. Track looked down at the snarling traffic. The rushing wind distorted his features and whipped at his clothes.

The helicopter was settling, six feet over the rear car now, as George shouted, "He says do it now!"

Track jumped, seeing a blur as Rafe Minor jumped, too. Track's feet impacted against the curved roof of the car. He spread-eagled himself with his hands splayed across the roof.

Track twisted around. Minor was slightly behind and beside him.

Track shouted at him. "Remember, six of them, probably only with handguns. But they're desperate. If they believed me, they already know they're dead, and if they didn't—"

"Hey, man, like a rumble in the old days—only you and me on the same side for once, huh?"

Track grinned as he started to crawl toward the rest of the car.

He looked skyward, but the helicopter was out of sight. His fingers reached for the edge of the roof, pulling him toward it. There was no way to guard against some of the six bombers waiting for him there, so he swung his left leg down. When his leg didn't get shot off, Track figured it was okay, and he swung the rest of his body down and in. His face was just above the train car's roof as he glanced forward. The purplish gray of the skyline for the Chicago Loop was ahead of him.

Track dropped to the platform, snaking the SPAS 12 from behind his back and flicking the safety off. He pushed off the trigger-guard safety, his back against the wall flanking the door leading into the car.

He could see Rafe Minor's feet now. Track glanced at his watch—maybe eight minutes, he guessed.

Rafe Minor cleared the roof and was down, his Aimpoint Sighted Colt M-16 sliding forward, Minor working the bolt. "We go?"

"Tell the civilians we're cops, it'll make it easier," Track said, trying the door handle. It didn't open.

Minor crashed the butt of the M-16 against it; the glass cracked but didn't shatter.

Track pushed the SPAS 12 out of the way and snatched out the Metalife Custom L-Frame .357. "Look out for a ricochet," he said to Minor, firing at the lock mechanism.

Minor reached out to the lock, quickly drawing his hand back. "Hot," Track observed, then turned half right, kicking his left heel back at it. The door lock fell away. Minor opened the door toward them and went through, with Track stepping in behind him. "Police!" Rafe Minor shouted. "Everybody get back!"

Track reholstered the L-Frame. Then he flicked the safety off the riot shotgun, pointing it ahead of him. He started down the center aisle as Minor took up the drag spot, Minor's M-16 traversing the car from right to left and back again.

Track reached the end of the car. He tried the door there and it opened effortlessly.

He stepped onto the platform, then jumped to the next car platform. The rail was a blur under him. He started to open the rear door of the car. The glass shattered, and Track dodged left and back, shouting, "Look out, Rafe!"

Track looked to the right. Two trains were stopped at a siding track. The police were working it now, sidetracking other trains, clearing the rails. Track looked above him through the break between the two car roofs. He saw a police helicopter moving through the blue gray sky.

"Never thought I'd be fightin' for the cops," Rafe Minor shouted over the clicking of wheels against the steel rails and the hiss of the slipstream.

"You ready? Make it two guns at least. The shots were too fast for aimed fire out of a conventional single gun."

"Gotcha." Minor nodded.

Track reached under the window frame. More shots. Shattered glass sprayed his leather-jacketed left arm. He twisted the door handle, swinging the door back and out toward him, then ducking beside it. More gunfire poured through the open doorway. The glass opposite them—the front door of the last car—disintegrated.

Track pushed the SPAS out on its sling, tensioned against him. He fired the riot shotgun through the doorway, hoping there were no passengers being used as shields. If there had been, he reasoned, they were dead.

He prayed there hadn't been.

He triggered another shot from the SPAS as he raced through the doorway, throwing himself down between two seats. Rafe Minor ran through firing the M-16 as Track looked up.

Two men were at the far end of the car, which was otherwise empty.

"Spray them with that M-16, Rafe!" Track shouted, pumping the trigger of the SPAS 12. Beside him, hot brass from the blazing M-16 pelted his neck and face. The roar of the shotgun deafened him. The volley from the two guns chewed up the seat backs as the two armed men at the front of the car went down, their guns silent.

The SPAS 12 was empty, and Track had no more ammo for it.

He unslung the riot shotgun and set it down on one of the seats. He drew out the L-Frame .357 and the Trapper Scorpion .45. The Scorpion was in his left, the revolver in his right.

Minor was cranking a new magazine into the M-16. Track stopped at the forward section of the car. There were two cars ahead—the second, the lead car. The bomb would be there—Track could feel it.

He didn't bother checking his watch; if there was enough time and he and Rafe had enough skill, the bombers would be stopped, the bomb itself defused. If there wasn't, counting seconds wouldn't help.

"Ready?" Track asked his friend.

"Ready, man." Minor kicked the door outward, firing a burst from the M-16 through the glass in the door, jumping across between the two cars, framing himself beside the door. Track followed him.

Buildings shot past them; the train lurched crazily. The clicking of the wheels against the rails sounded louder now.

Track stuck the revolver in his waistband—then reached for the door handle, twisting it and pushing the door open toward Rafe. Drawing out the .357 again, Track waited, both pistols in his hands.

Minor shoved the M-16 through the door and fired a long burst. Track shouted, "Get down everybody, below the seats." Then he dived under the muzzle-flashes of the assault rifle, half rolling and coming up on his knees. A single gunman at the end of the car was firing an autoloading pistol. Passengers on both sides of Track screamed as the pistols in his hands boomed. Track heard Minor yell, "Dan, I'm hit!" Track kept on shooting at the gunman. His body danced as each slug hit him. Then he went down, back against the window in the door behind him, shattering the glass with his head. The door flew open, and the body slipped from sight.

Track jammed the revolver in his belt, running forward. Passengers shrank from him. Track shouted, "Rafe, can you walk?"

"Yeah, but my tailor ain't gonna be too pleased."

Track loaded a fresh magazine into the Scorpion. Then he speed-loaded the L-Frame with one of the Safariland Loaders and closed the cylinder. The spent shells were under his feet as he stopped at the open doorway.

He looked back. Rafe Minor was limping, his left thigh soaked with blood. Rafe's hands reloaded the M-16.

Track took the Trapper into his left hand, the Metalife .357 in his right. "Ready? This is the big one . . . three of them . . . the bomb . . . the whole ball of wax."

"Let's do it," Rafe said, shoving the M-16 through the open doorway. He fired a burst through the far-door window glass, aiming high to avoid hitting any bystanders, Track realized.

Track dodged through the open doorway, jumping across the gap between the cars. They were out of the Loop—the factories and old tenements around him now—heading into the West Side and the western suburbs.

The end of the line was near.

The irony of the thought struck him as he watched Rafe Minor hobble across, slowed by the leg wound.

"Like last time, Dan?"

"Yeah, like last time . . . only way," Track said, looking up. The blue-and-white helicopter hovered on one side of the train, two police choppers on the other side.

A loud-hailer was sounding. "Aboard the train, lay down your arms and surrender, this is the police!"

A helicopter skimmed near the train, then away. A man with a sniper rifle fired, shattering the glass beside Track's head.

"Shit!" Minor snarled. "They shootin' at us, man!"

"Must think we're terrorists."

"Right," said Rafe, edging back.

Track worked the door handle, letting the door fly open. "Get down!" he shouted as Minor fired a burst through the door.

Gunfire seemed to pour through the open doorway as Rafe fired inside and the three gunmen fired back. Track threw himself into the car, flat onto the aisle. His right thigh stopped a slug as he tried to cram his body behind a seat back. A pretty black girl was huddled there, her eyes wide with fear. "Relax, we're the good guys," Track said, looking away from her at his leg. It wasn't a bleeder and the leg still moved.

He twisted around, extending his left hand past the seat back, firing the Scorpion .45, emptying the magazine, then tucking back.

Gunfire ripped into the seat back above him, dimpling the metal backing. Glass in the windows near him shattered.

He dumped the spent magazine, loading a second spare—his last—and chambering the first round.

Minor was still outside the door.

"Hold it," Track shouted. "Hold it, Rafe!"

Track sucked in his breath. "Hey, you guys! Krieger was lying. He always lies. The bomb's going off in a minute or so, maybe less—"

"You're a liar!"

"That toggle switch you've got to flick—whatever it is—that's a fake timer—doesn't do anything!"

"Liar!" came another voice.

"You'll burn up, dead. Mass murderers and committing suicide at the same time. We can defuse the bomb, maybe. Give it up...run if you want—I don't want you. I want to defuse the bomb."

"The National Socialist Movement shall be victorious," another voice shouted, clear, bell-like. Track gritted his teeth.

"Asshole!" Track spat the word as he got to his feet, firing both pistols, shouting, "Now, Rafe, now!"

Track's Metalife Custom blew off the head of a man holding a Hi-Power. Hot brass pelted Track as the M-16 started to chatter; another of the three men went down. His pistol discharged into the ceiling as he spun, danced, then dropped.

Track was moving forward shoulder to shoulder with Rafe Minor. Both men were firing; Track's .45 pistol was spitting brass. The gunfire was deafening as the last man—his body cut to ribbons—fell forward, a pistol in each hand.

There was more screaming.

Track's guns were empty.

The M-16 had stopped.

The seconds were ticking away faster than the clicking of the wheels on the steel rails.

Track started forward toward the engineer's compartment ahead of them. He ripped open the door. The engineer was shot in the neck; the wound was sucking and pumping. "This guy's still alive."

"Get him out. I'll find the bomb," Rafe Minor gasped.

Track nodded, pulling the man from his round metal stool, easing him to the seat opposite. Track almost tripped over the body of one of the Nazi terrorists. He looked through a shot-out window; they were nearly into Oak Park. At the speed they were going, they were on a direct collision course with the switchyard.

He looked on the floor of the control booth at the metal pedal with rubber treads. It was pressed hard against the floor. He reached down to try to release it. It was a deadman's switch and should work. He tried to pry it up with his fingers, but it wouldn't budge. "I don't know what they did to this," Track shouted.

"Never mind that, I found the bomb," Minor shouted.

Track left the jammed pedal alone, shouting across the car, "We can't stop the train. We need an orderly evacuation to the next car. Then we can uncouple it—"

People were screaming and running, pushing past Rafe Minor and the trunk-sized piece of luggage with the bomb in it.

Track found a fresh speedloader for the L-Frame and rammed it into place, closing the cylinder, double-actioning two rounds into the ceiling.

There was a scream, then silence.

"Order, dammit! Now get into the next car and stay there. We've got a bomb to defuse! I'll shoot the first bastard that runs or pushes!"

Track pocketed the empty speedloader.

"I got the cowling off. . . the timer—"

Track moved forward, letting the passengers move around him as he dropped to his knees beside Rafe. The timer showed an LED readout in red numerals—eighty-seven seconds.

"We'll never—"

"Get into the wiring," Track rasped, helping as Minor pried at the rest of the cowling. It popped free.

Facing them was a sea of wires of almost every color.

"Oh, man, this is like what they gave us in school—double blinds, blinds, false detonator triggers, the whole shot. It'll take a bomb-disposal team twenty years to figure this out! Here, this one—" And Rafe Minor clipped a wire with his pocket knife against his thumb. But the timer kept running. "That shoulda been it. Hell—I—"

"Try another one—we have nothing to lose," Track shouted.

"But which one? Jeez—"

Track reached past him; Minor stayed his hands. "Man, you'll blow us all up!"

Track looked at the timer—forty-one seconds.

"We'll die, anyway."

"Wait—" Minor moved his hands over the wires, saying almost to himself, "If this dude was so damn tricky, maybe he did the ultimate trick, the obvious thing—naw—"

"What?" Track growled.

"Just turn off the switch for the damn timer. Only a joker, a crazy guy'd do that."

Track reached for the switch, his eyes locking with Rafe Minor's. "If it ain't, we're dead," Minor told him.

Track shrugged, his right thumb over the switch. He flipped it down. The timer stopped—three seconds.

Track rolled back the cuff of his jacket, watched his Rolex's second hand sweep—two seconds, one second—

Nothing happened.

Minor almost screamed like a woman. "Hey, we're alive!"

Track looked up. The train station they were passing read Oak Park Avenue.

Track pushed himself to his feet. "The hell we are. Less than a mile and this train slams into whatever's in the railyard!"

"I got the bomb," Rafe Minor shouted.

Track said nothing, lurching toward the body of the still-breathing driver. He grabbed at the man's shoulders and hauled him up, blood spurting from his neck wound across Track's hands. Track's own right leg pained him as he bent his right shoulder into the man, picking him up, slinging him across his back.

Minor was shouting, "I got your gun, too!" Minor was limping. The suitcase with the bomb was under his left arm, while his right hand supported it.

Track shouted, "When we get across, I'm going to uncouple this thing and you find the brake for the next car back."

"Right!"

Track glanced through a shot-out window. They were passing into the Marion Street station—three or four blocks.

Rafe was through the door, with Track behind him. He threw the unconscious man into the arms of Rafe Minor, who'd set down the bomb.

Track bent between the cars, looking at the tangle of wires and cables.

He took out his Puma folding knife, flicking it open and hacking at the wires. Then he stopped, placing the knife between his teeth.

Marion Street was to his left. "Shit!"

He reached down to the chains between the cars, popping them, then to the coupling bolt. The wires would break, he told himself.

He jerked at the coupling bolt—it was stuck. He jerked again—it moved a little.

He jerked again—it was out. The first car lurched ahead, the cables breaking, sparks of electricity flying. Track threw himself back, looking through the open doorway, climbing to his knees. Rafe Minor was half in the engineer's box; his right leg had vanished inside it.

Track staggered as the train jumped and bucked

under him. Passengers were screaming. Track fell to his
face, his knife clattering to the floor. He looked behind
him, ahead down the tracks.

The lead car was going past the Harlem station to the
train yard ahead. The lead car was speeding into it, impacting, skyrocketing upward as metal fragments and
glass sprayed up everywhere. Track could hear the tearing and crunching of steel as the train climbed the one it
had plowed into, flipping up and over like a performing
dolphin. The train car smashed into a fuel tanker, and a
yellow-and-black fireball belched upward with a roar.

Track covered his ears. The train under him rocked
and bumped, its passengers screaming. He turned
around, taking his hands from his ears. The screams
grew louder. There was a violent shudder.

The train had stopped.

Track remembered to breathe.

There was more screaming, and he looked around.

Three policemen in flak vests stood above him, M-16s
in their hands, the muzzles inches from his head. Track,
still on his knees, looked up into their faces and laughed.
"You know, I can explain all this. No kidding!"

31

The fire was what they always called "roaring" in books, Track thought.

Dorothy climbed onto his lap as he sat with his feet up in the Stratolounger, watching the flames. He had a warm feeling inside—not from the fire, but from the telephone conversation. Desiree Goth had said he'd got her out of bed.

He had told her he never wanted to do that, then the conversation had continued.

"I still love you, Dan. When will I see you?"

"Soon. I've got a project I need some help with—right up your alley—tracking down some stolen weapons."

"*The* stolen weapons?"

"You've got good contacts."

"How many?" she asked.

"Ninety-nine remaining."

"You know what I'll do if I get them? Sell them to third-world nations.... I could retire."

"You're too young to retire. Anyway, help me get them, then Zulu and I can fight it out to see who keeps them."

"Okay," she agreed, laughing.

"How is Zulu, anyway?"

"Stronger than ever."

"Great. I'm leaving tomorrow. There's a stopover in New York. Then I'll be in Europe the day after."

"Why don't you come and see me?"

"All right," he told her.

Then they had both hung up.

Sir Abner interrupted his thoughts. "I say, Dan?"

"Yes?"

"No chance, I suppose, well, that Krieger plans to detonate those things one at a time?"

"What?" Track looked up at him. Chesterton was smoking a pipe and leaning against the fireplace, a drink on the mantel beside him.

"He'll try to blow up one or two, then tell us what he wants," Track said with a sigh.

He sipped at his own drink—Seagrams Seven and ice. His right leg was a little stiff, his throat a little sore from question answering, too. The toughest questions had been from Miles Jefferson and his FBI team. But Jefferson had left, promising to punch Track out if Track interfered again.

Track didn't take Jefferson seriously—he was always losing his temper. Track thought he'd see him again.

He heard footsteps and glanced across the room.

"Well, how do I look? Come on, be honest."

It was George, wearing a gray three-piece suit, hair neatly combed.

"Terrific."

"Like the proverbial ladykiller, dear boy."

Track looked over at Chesterton, who was smiling. "Well, got to be off. The plane's picking me up in two hours. I have some last-minute details to attend to. I'll see both of you in New York." Chesterton pushed away from the fireplace and started across the room as

Track's eyes followed him. "And George, good luck on that date with Tassles LaToure. Don't do anything I wouldn't do."

A horn honked. Track stood up, pushing the footrest down. Dorothy jumped from his lap.

Track walked to the door and gazed out. He recognized Tassles La Toure's car.

"Hey, George, she's early—"

"Blocked my car," Chesterton said, peering out beside Track. "Afraid you'll have to go first, George."

"Hey, but do I look okay?" George asked.

Track patted his nephew on the shoulder. "Terrific, George."

"Funny she didn't want me to pick her up."

"Had a near-miss auto accident once a few years back. She's always driven herself since then."

"Well, I'll change her mind on that." George beamed, starting through the door.

"Hey," Track advised. "Look, you take it easy. That arm's still bandaged and—"

"I know. I'll be easy." George, his left hand swathed in bandages, slipped through the door into the night.

Track looked out, shouting after him, "Remember, early tomorrow. We have to leave for the Big Apple!"

Chesterton started through the door, then stopped, peering out into the night. Track followed his gaze, watching as George walked down the driveway toward the car.

"I say, Dan, I think, well, sending a twenty-five-year-old out with a striptease artist—really—"

"Look, he's a big guy. He'll handle her."

Chesterton nodded on his way out.

"Good night," Track called after him, closing the door and locking it.

He walked back across the room, sat down in the Stratolounger beside the fire and took a sip of his drink. Dorothy jumped into his lap again, purring.

His gaze fell on the cigarette burn on the arm of the Stratolounger. He remembered that one of the guests had put it there when Track had thrown the surprise party three months or so back—the one for Tassles LaToure's sixty-third birthday.

AHERN ON AHERN

I started banging out adventure stories on an old typewriter when I was about ten years old, and I quickly found out that getting published was like trying to hit a home run with a toothpick.

I decided that if publishers wouldn't willingly consider my stories, I'd have to apply some force. The single greatest asset a writer can have is determination. That's something I've always held to be a vital element of a person's life, and something I've tried to put into all the characters in my books.

I was lucky, and was able to combine my love of writing with a lifelong interest in guns. Since 1973 I've written more than five hundred articles on guns, guns and more guns. I still actively free-lance gun articles, test the latest handguns and continue research on the subject.

Hard-won success in the adventure-fiction field didn't come until I was in my thirties with the publication of two series—*They Call Me the Mercenary* and *The Survivalist*. You might say that it only took me twenty-five years to become an "overnight success."

I could not have achieved all that I have without the help of my co-writer, co-conspirator, photographer, lifelong buddy and best friend—my wife Sharon Ahern. Together with Sharon and our two children, Jason and Sammie, I enjoy life on an estate in northeastern Georgia, doing what I like for a living.

Coming soon

TRACK

#3 The Armageddon Conspiracy
by Jerry Ahern

"Score a million points to survive . . ."

At the top of the video screen, tiny yellow helicopters were swarming like hungry insects looking for blood.

"Thirty seconds and then bye-bye! This is the final attack!" The voice of Klaus Gurnheim, Krieger's mad bomber, gloated over the speaker.

Gurnheim had taken a perverse pleasure in hooking a video game up to the detonation device he had wired into the nuclear warhead. He had gambled that this would be one skill Track didn't possess. What he hadn't counted on was a twelve-year-old schoolboy muscling forward to grab the joystick out of Track's hands.

The video laser whined, and a light beam ripped across the screen at the advancing death choppers. They needed to vaporize just one more to master the game and, Gurnheim had promised, disarm the bomb. But could they trust the word of a psychopath and a liar?

"Three seconds," came Gurnheim's triumphant voice.

Jason swiveled the joystick and zeroed in on his target.

One second. The image on the screen started to fade.

"Shoot! Shoot!" Track yelled.
